Musical Moment

MUSICAL MOMENT

and other stories

❁

YEHOSHUA KENAZ

STEERFORTH PRESS

SOUTH ROYALTON, VERMONT

For information about permission to reproduce selections
from this book, write to: Steerforth Press L.C., P.O. Box 70,
South Royalton, Vermont 05068.

First published in Hebrew 1980 by Ha'kibbutz Hameuchad, Tel Aviv.

An excerpt from the poem "Letter" by Nathan Alterman, which appears
in "Between Night and Dawn," was originally published in Hebrew in
Nathan Alterman, *Collected Works*, vol. 1 (Ha'kibbutz Hameuchad,
Tel Aviv, 1971) and translated by Robert Friend.

Library of Congress Cataloging-in-Publication Data
Kenaz, Yehoshu'a.
[Moment musikali. English]
Musical moment : and other stories / Yehoshua Kenaz.
p.   cm.
ISBN 1-883642-18-3. — ISBN 1-883642-47-7 (pbk.)
I. Title.
PJ5054.K36M6613   1995
892.4'36—dc20   95-4306

Manufactured in the United States of America

First North American Edition

Contents

✸

The Three-Legged Chicken

❃

translated from the hebrew by dalya bilu

One day at the end of summer they laid the old man they called grandfather on the floor in the big room, lit candles at his head and closed the double doors on him and on the people standing around him. The last rays of sun filtered through the colored panes of glass at the tops of the windows and the veranda door to say their last farewells, staining the walls, the floor and the body with violet, green and orange lights and making the flames of the candles look very thin and pale in comparison.

When his mother emerged from the big room she stood opposite the boy and bent over him, bringing her face level with his so that she could say what she had to say to him in a very soft voice. She smiled for a moment, a strange smile that he had never seen on her face before, and he did not know if it was anxiety or malice glittering in her eyes when she said to him: our grandfather is dead, our grandfather is dead—but it was obvious to him that she knew she was hurting him for nothing, and that this was what she wanted, and in this matter there would be no concessions.

He asked when his father was coming, because he knew that at a time like this his father was bound to come and restore order and security, but there was no reply. The old man they called grandfather, who used to come every evening when the boy got into bed, to urge and beg him again and again to say "Hear Oh Israel," if only for his sake, did not come to his room that night, just as he had not come on any of the previous evenings of his brief and final illness. And knowing this, he wanted to say "Hear Oh Israel" to make him happy, to repeat the words after him as he wished him to do and to give him love in return for the love he gave him.

All night long it seemed as if people were walking about on tiptoe in the rooms and passages of the house in the dark, seeking, secretly laboring at all kinds of tasks whose meaning there was no way of knowing. For hours the boy racked his memory for the words of the prayer which had suddenly vanished, as if the old man had taken them with him on his journey. For hours he could not fall asleep, and no one came to the doorway to peep into his room and see how he was. All night long he waited for his father to arrive home from work and to hear his voice and know that he had someone to take care of him. Until late at night the quiet bustle continued, and when the searching and silent prowling between the rooms ended there were only the brief, businesslike whispers of people parting from each other for a while until they met again to set out on a journey together.

And when silence fell the boy heard the voice of the woodworm again, friend of the sleepless, burrowing in the depths of the old wardrobes, laboring and pausing in her labors and beginning her nibbling again, momentarily taking fright and listening to the sound of his breathing in order to ascertain that it was rhythmic and he was indeed asleep: and if not—she would stop and make an effort not to disturb him and wait until he fell asleep; but no sooner had she conquered her drive for a moment than it would reassert itself and overwhelm her with its strength. And the boy would outwit her and restrain his breath. And the worm would wonder if he had really fallen asleep and she could go ahead without anything to stop her, and she would send out tentative signals, groping in the dark. Very hesitantly she would venture an experimental nibble, nibbling and stopping, afraid of exaggerating, trying to discover how much she could dare at once without bringing wrath and catastrophe down on her head. She was so full of a sense of the significance of the deed she was destined to do, and so full of the prudence demanded by the importance of the task and the need to perform it stealthily, obsequiously, and ingenuously. And nevertheless, as soon as she plucked up courage, or simply succumbed to her drive and went back to work, she would be overcome by an urgent, panic-stricken need to cram as much as she could into one short moment, in order to make up for the time lost in the pause of the past and counteract the paralysis that would take hold of her a moment later, when her senses were alerted to the danger again. With blind enthusiasm she would plunge into her labors, the other possibility receding as she did so, and until the fear came back again she would accomplish whatever she could. And when she stopped, it was obvious that she was in the grip of terror and great remorse, and that she was playing a cunning game of deceit and make-believe: clinging tightly to her place, shrinking into herself as far as she could, and pretending to be bodiless and spaceless, a concentrated point of alertness to spy out the silence. And whenever she stopped work for longer than usual, breaking the accustomed rhythm, the boy would cover his face silently with the sheet and roll his whole body into it, very slowly, so that not the slightest sound would reach her, and he would lie motionless, barely breathing and imagining that he, too, was all closed in and wrapped up in himself, and since his eyes were closed his bed turned into one of the deepest, most hidden veins of the wood, shrouded in eternal darkness, warm and protective, and thus he and she would listen to each other in the silence, and she would always be the first to give in to the illusion of safety, send out a tentative, experimental signal, a tiny sound to test the reaction: and since nothing happened to arouse her suspicions that a trap was being set for her in the silence, and since her appetite had been whetted and her passion had blinded her to all sense of caution and danger, she would fall to work again. And sometimes she would go on for longer than usual in her enthusiasm and oblivion, and the boy would wonder how far this eagerness of hers would deafen her to the danger signals from outside. After a long moment during which she did not stop he would cough loudly and she would fall silent immediately, and her silence would go on and on, as if it were taking her a long time to recover from her terror.

At that moment the boy remembered the big room and the old man they called grandfather, who had been left there by himself. He opened his eyes and suddenly the sounds of the night broke into his room from outside: the sound of crickets rising from the furthest reaches of the house and the yard, and the chorus of frogs gathered by the cowshed and in the garden, and the howling of the jackals in the citrus groves—all these silenced the soundless game between his breathing and the whispering of the woodworm, and with them the ample light of the moon came flooding into the room. And since he was accustomed to this pattern of sounds and its regular sequence, he did not even raise his head from the pillow to see what was happening around him. The shadow of the oil lamp standing at the end of the passage stretched like a long dark triangle from the threshold of his room to a corner of the house which was invisible from where he was lying. And he wanted to get up and see what was in the big room at this hour of night, but his body refused to respond to his will, as if it had been turned to stone.

From all the corners of the room the dark and loathsome thing advanced on him. He opened his mouth to scream, but his lips and voice were paralyzed, and only the muscles of his throat strained to call for help or break the evil spell of the moment, but in vain. He felt that he was not dreaming, but this was how he always felt when the thing came at him out of the dark, and only in the morning, when he recalled it to his memory, he would wonder if he had been dreaming or if he had really been awake when he saw it. And only the vestiges of the scream that he had wanted to utter but couldn't remained like a painful sensation in his throat.

In the morning he would get up and look for the trickle of powder that had fallen from the wardrobe, the worm's nightly work and a concrete proof that those moments were real, and he would crumble the powder between his fingers until it disintegrated and was absorbed into his skin, and much as he wanted to derive some secret knowledge from it and its touch, all his efforts were in vain.

The quilt and mattress renovator sat on an empty crate next to one of the citrus groves and took a hard-boiled egg, about a quarter of a loaf of black bread and a few olives and tomatoes out of the little haversack slung over his shoulder and got ready to eat his breakfast. The instrument he used to tease the cotton wool, which resembled a big harp with one string, stood leaning against the fence and at its foot a bundle of tools tied up in a coarse cloth of a blue-gray color. There was not a soul to be seen and the only sound was the murmur of the water in the irrigation canals coming from the citrus groves. It was already quite late in the morning. The quilt and mattress renovator took the egg and aimed it at the middle of his forehead. Although there was no audience to witness his tricks he could not suppress the buffoonery which in the course of plying his trade had become second nature to him. He held the egg opposite his forehead, squinted at it with both eyes, moved it away again, with his eyes squinting at it all the time as if in alarmed anticipation of the blow which was about to descend at any minute, and which indeed materialized immediately as the man smashed the egg on his forehead and burst out laughing. He held the egg with its shattered shell in his left hand and started removing the bits of white shell very slowly and meticulously. When he had finished he inspected it carefully to see if there were any bits left. His face was serious now, but his eyes hinted to the empty sun-washed spaces in front of him that there was one more joke in store for them: again he squinted at his nose and all at once he dropped the whole peeled egg into his wide open mouth, where it vanished without a trace. He looked about him as if to test the reaction of his nonexistent audience and then slapped his cheeks with both hands, as if to hit the egg from one side of his mouth to the other, like a tennis ball. After this his shoulders heaved convulsively, as if he had swallowed the whole egg. Then he spat it out into the palm of his hand, took a few olives from the handkerchief spread out in front of him, stuck his teeth into the quarter loaf of black bread and started chewing with his mouth open, while at the same time humming a cheerful tune and swaying his head from side to side in time with the tune.

Two men appeared at the end of the road, one of them carrying a suitcase and the other a kind of square box covered with a sack, and began advancing towards the quilt and mattress renovator. When they reached the place where he was sitting they stopped and exchanged a few words with him. Then they consulted with each other, put the suitcase and the sack-covered box down on the ground, sat down next to the man, and began to roll themselves cigarettes. They rolled one for him too. The three of them smoked peacefully in almost total silence.

The two men lay back on the ground, rested their heads on their hands and closed their eyes. The quilt and mattress renovator kept darting glances at the sack-covered box and an ugly smile appeared on his face, as if he had remembered an obscene joke. Then he looked at the two sleeping men and his face suddenly fell. He stared at the fields and citrus groves and his eyes scanned the dirt road beside which he was sitting, which twisted and turned and receded into the distance until it disappeared around a corner next to the horizon. He remembered to cast a glance from time to time at his one-stringed harp and his bundle of tools, but he would immediately turn his head away and start staring into space again, and there was a great sadness in his eyes. He too would have liked to lie back like them and take a nap, but since he had promised them to look after their things until they had recovered their strength he did not stir from his place, nor did he dare to hum his songs for fear of disturbing their sleep.

When the two men rose after a little while he asked them to take him with them, and they laughed at him. They pointed at his tools and he promised that he would sell them and give the proceeds to the men, or even abandon them where they lay and follow them with no more ado. He took their hands and begged them, saying that he would do anything for them if only they would let him join them. They laughed. They straightened their clothes. One of them picked up the suitcase and the other the box covered with the sack, and the quilt and mattress renovator called out to them. They set out. He leapt up and ran after them.

They did not turn their heads and he walked along behind them. Until the man with the suitcase picked up a stone and threatened to throw it at him; but still he was not deterred. And seeing that the man was still following them and that he was already far away from the citrus grove and the fence where he had left his tools lying, they stopped and turned to face him. The man with the suitcase picked up a stone again and this time he threw it with all his strength at the quilt and mattress renovator and hit his leg. He jumped into the air as if he had been bitten by a snake and then stood rooted to the spot again. They continued on their way without turning their heads again, and he yelled curses and entreaties and abuse after them. Until they disappeared from view and he returned unwillingly to the place where he had left his tools. He sat down on the crate and began humming his songs and staring into space again.

In the morning they sent a cart to the ice factory to fetch ice and the boy did not know what they wanted the ice for. His uncle, his mother's brother, stood in the back yard facing the cowshed, and he looked at him for a long time without saying a word. The sound of the Arab playing his fiddle drifted out of the dark doorway together with the smell of the cows and their fodder. No one had told the Arab to stop playing his fiddle. His uncle called the boy to him softly, gave him a few coins and told him to go to the little market to buy the newspapers. They wanted to see how the funeral notices had been printed. And the boy really wanted to stay and wait for his father to come, and to see when the cart came and what they would do with the ice and if they would leave any of it unguarded. But the people who up to that day had belonged to him were now busy with their own affairs. And also the old man they called grandfather who, during the boy's illness, had prowled restlessly around his bed, sighing bitterly and bringing him glasses of lukewarm water sweetened with sugar to sweeten the pill of his sickness a little, and saying indulgent things to him in a broken voice with his peculiar accent, and stroking his forehead with a heavy, hesitant hand—he too had joined the conspiracy and lay motionless on the floor in the big room with candles burning at his head, waiting for the blocks of ice they had sent the cart to bring for him for a purpose the boy could not fathom.

His father was working then in one of the army camps near Haifa and came only for Saturdays. On Friday evenings the boy would go and stand in the street long before the time his mother told him to, waiting to see the figure of his father appearing in the distance and coming toward him from the top of the road, to examine his face and his body and touch his clothes that had come from far away and get to know him anew all over again and wait for him to throw him into the air and hug him. His father had not yet come but he knew that he would come, even though it wasn't Friday evening.

He put the money in his trouser pocket and went to put on his sandals.

That morning they brought Bruria home for the summer vacation from school, which was far away from the town. Her mother and father got up early in the morning so that they would have time to bring her back and take her home before too many people saw her. When the bus arrived Bruria refused to get off until her parents promised to buy her new shoes. She was wearing laced-up boots and her parents tried to persuade her that these boots were healthier for her feet and prevented them from getting tired. But Bruria stamped her feet and said that she would not budge from her place in the bus until they promised to buy her the most modern high heeled shoes, and in Tel Aviv, nowhere but Tel Aviv would do. All the way from the bus station to their house next to the little market they kept her quiet with arguments and promises: Whoever buys new shoes just like that on an ordinary day in the middle of the year? On Passover Eve we'll buy you new shoes. And anyway the ones you've got on are still new, they look as if they've just come out of the shop. —When's Passover eve? asked Bruria. —It'll be here soon. In a little while. —After these holidays? asked Bruria. —Yes, said her father. —After the winter? —Yes, said her father. Bruria reflected for a moment and her father said: But only if you're good and do what you're told and listen to your mother and don't talk to people.

Passover Eve, said Bruria, Passover Eve, Passover Eve. After the summer and after the winter. In a little while. Soon. And in Tel Aviv, in the most modern shop? And thus she gave in to them and went home with them, dreaming about her new shoes. But as soon as they got there she forgot all about their promises and sat down on the sofa and scowled angrily at her big boots. —What's gotten into your head about your shoes? Did somebody at school say something about them? asked her mother. But Bruria did not reply, only stamped her feet in hatred and humiliation and then fell furiously on her boots, quickly undoing the laces and taking them off and hurling them into a corner of the room. Afterward she took her socks off too and sat barefoot. Her father said to her: If you don't behave yourself we'll take you back to school and we won't buy you new shoes on Passover Eve or ever in all your life.

When the boy went into the street there was still no sign of the cart returning from the ice factory. He saw Molcho sitting next to the notice board and whispering something to himself, as if he were hatching some evil. Molcho was hostile to the boy because of some forgotten quarrel, or perhaps there had never been a quarrel at all and the boy had simply walked past his house on the street of the Sephardim and Molcho had tried to hit him. And when he saw him coming Molcho stood up and started shaking the dust from his trousers. He gave the boy a hard look and his lips were parted in a challenging smile. The boy started walking without looking at him. But he imagined he could hear Molcho's bare feet padding behind him like some wild cat, and he knew that the moment he heard them quicken he would run away as fast as he could. But as long as he kept on padding softly behind him he wouldn't anger him by sudden flight. He concentrated all his senses on listening and on the effort to check the flight begging to break out in his feet and keep them on the alert so as not to miss the moment when it would become necessary to bound forward and run. For a moment it seemed to him that he no longer heard the bare feet padding behind him but he was afraid to turn his head and look. Until he gathered up his courage and looked and saw Molcho standing a few steps behind him and beckoning him to approach. But the boy did not budge. —Come on, I won't hit you, said Molcho. The boy approached. —Your grandfather's dead, said Molcho. —It's not true, said the boy: Who said so? —I'll hit you if you lie, said Molcho. And the boy said nothing. —They've brought Bruria home for the holidays, said Molcho. I saw her. He looked for a moment at the windows of the house, and since there was nothing to see he turned his back on the boy and walked away. The boy let him go, and when he was about to turn into the little market to buy the newspapers he heard her voice calling him from the window: Little boy, little boy, come here for a minute.

He went into the yard and stood facing the window. He saw her face, the face of a pretty child, pale, dark-eyed, and her hair which was already full of gray streaks. —Don't be frightened little boy, you can come into the house, my mother and father have gone out and I'm alone, said Bruria. But he stayed where he was and went on looking at her face. In the window frame she looked like a figure in a portrait, from the waist up. She leaned with her elbows on the sill, one hand dangling and tapping the wall and the other patting her hair into place. —On Passover Eve they're going to buy me new shoes, in Tel Aviv, the most modern shoes there are! With high heels. She fell silent for a moment and closed her eyes. There was a triumphant smile on her pale, pretty face: And at night I'll dance with all the boys! And I'll be the belle of the ball! And I'll dance with the boys all night long!

Opposite the big tap next to the cowshed, in the back yard of my house, a long time before, before all the times I have ever known, I experienced something like an awakening from a dream into a new dream. I always spent a lot of time sitting opposite the big tap and playing with it, because the handle of the tap had been removed to stop it from dripping, and also perhaps to prevent me from opening it and playing with the water as I loved to do. But I kept plugging away and never gave up trying to open it with stones and bits of wire, nails, and even my teeth.

Until I resigned myself at last and passed my fingers over the thick, cold pipe, seeking something to take hold of, some secret catch which would make everything work like magic. The cowshed with the two steps at its door and the dim light inside it always looked blurred, and the Arab sat inside it playing his fiddle.

And as I sat stroking the stem of the tap a great and mysterious spirit passed over me, over me and the world around me: the wall of the cowshed and the two steps took on before my eyes their final, definitive form, and the strains of the Arab's fiddle emerging from the doorway sounded as if they were coming from the bowels of the earth. And the earth steaming with a pleasant warmth and the dusty sky and the wooden fence and the trough and the little back shed next to the urinal and the smell of the cows and the sourness of the sacks of fodder and the flock of birds suddenly startled into flight from the roof of the cowshed, shooting like an arrow of little black dashes to the tops of the trees and from there to the limits of the horizon: the more fixed and formed and self-sufficient they became the further they receded from me, shrouded in strangeness and perhaps even hostility. And at the same time—from unknown depths inside me—there rose a voice, and the voice said: I, I, I, I. And although the voice came from inside me, it wasn't my voice. And the voice was quiet, solemn, redeeming and very dangerous, and it stiffened my hand on the chilly metal of the big tap, which had become rounder and more slippery, trying to shake my fingers off and put an end to all my games. And the voice filled me with dread and a joy whose cause I could not tell, but I felt that it was greater than I was. Out of the twilight silence the voice spoke to me and I looked around me, tried to rise to my feet and could not, like at night in my bed when the dark, loathsome thing came at me from all the corners of the room. The vividness of the shapes awakening to a life of their own before my eyes and the painful and liberating current flowing through me, strong and silent, coming from an unknown source and spreading through all my limbs, brought the scent of the greatest of all possible adventures before me. And the voice rising from the depths of my being pushed onto my lips the words which slipped out as silently as if it were not I saying them but a stranger sitting inside me and calling without stopping, in great astonishment: I, I, I, I.

A heavy load descended on my shoulders and squatted there, like an uninvited guest with the right to stay forever.

My hand fell from the snub-nosed tap and the Arab went on playing his fiddle inside the cowshed. The sound of the Arab's fiddle with its thin notes dragging out endlessly like the voice of some strange beast, heartbreaking in its sobbing, moaning its longings for other places, told me that from now on every step I took and everything I did and everything I touched would be a secret known only to me and never to be revealed to anyone else in the world. For my hands had touched the last wall of all—behind which there was nothing.

A hidden hand dragged Bruria away from the window and her cries rose from inside the house: Handsome boys and girls in party dresses are dancing together all night long, and I'm going to dance with them too!

And then the boy heard the sound of blows and Bruria screaming. Her old father came out onto the porch and approached the boy: What are you doing here, he asked, with your grandfather dead?!

She called me, said the boy.

Go home, said her father.

And he stood on the porch waiting for the boy to go. The sound of Bruria's shrieks rose from the house and her mother drew the blind and shut the window where Bruria had been standing before, as if she were in a picture.

When he went into the street the boy saw the little market in front of him and a crowd of people outside Yardeni's café. He approached the people and they told him that the three-legged chicken was on display inside the café. Two men, they said, had obtained the chicken on loan from its owners, who had brought it from abroad, and there was nothing like it anywhere in the world. The two of them were passing through the town on their way and they had agreed to stop for a few hours to put the monster on display. The next day they would leave for a tour of the surrounding towns and then they would take their show overseas. The sound of laughter rose from Yardeni's little café, which was packed with people. Strange, obscene cries were heard from the interior. The entrance fee, explained the people standing outside, was divided equally between the owner of the chicken, the two men traveling around with it, and Yardeni, who had made his café available for the show. The faces of the people emerging from the café after the five minutes paid for by the entrance fee were exhausted with laughter and astonishment. The boy drew nearer the doorway, pushing his way through the crowd of curiosity seekers and people waiting in line to pay the entrance fee. Suddenly he felt a hand on his shoulder and Molcho's face was very close to his, steaming with heat and smelling of sweat.

You want me to look after you? I'll look after you forever, just like my brother.

And Molcho did not cease clutching his shoulder.

A chicken, with three legs, said Molcho. It talks and dances and pulls faces.

The boy put his hands in his pockets and felt the coins and knew that he would not buy the newspapers which he had been sent to fetch and that he would never again see the face of the old man lying on the floor of the big room, and the cart they had sent to the ice factory, and a great anxiety swept through him and drew his heart toward unknown things. He stretched out his hand to Molcho's shoulder and clasped it in great fear.

And you can come and swing on the swing in our yard whenever you like, with my brother. He gave him the coins he had taken out of his pocket.

I'll look after you forever, said Molcho, even more than my brother.

The monster stood inside its little cage made of flimsy wooden slats, which had been placed on top of a high box. There was a handful of grain in the corner of the cage but she did not touch it. She kept rolling her eyes around and swiveling her head from side to side so as not to miss anything that was going on around her. And she would hop on her two healthy legs and jump backwards, as if she was trying to escape from the danger surrounding her on all sides, and her extra leg, her sick leg, stuck out behind her, defiant and provocative. Yardeni stood next to the cage guarding it against the blows of the people who were trying to tease the chicken and elicit grotesque and surprising reactions from her. And a certain cart driver, a very heavy man who always wore a sweaty cap on his head, kept circling his mouth with his hands like a trumpet and imitating a cock's crow in order to awaken her longings for a male and every movement she made would then be interpreted as a response to this simulated mating call, seductive and very obscene, giving rise to loud guffaws of laughter. The two men who had brought the chicken sat at a table next to the door and took the entrance fees. And every now and then Yardeni glanced in their direction to make sure that they weren't putting any of the money into their pockets before giving him his share.

The drunkard sat at his usual table in the corner, untouched by all the commotion. He was in a quiet and very thoughtful mood. And only when a very loud burst of laughter rose from the crowd around the cage, in reaction to one of the spectator's comments or one of the monster's movements, the drunk would raise his eyes, shake his head dismissively, and whisper: Vanity of vanities, vanity of vanities.

There was a bad smell in the crowded café, and the boy did not connect it with the congestion and the sweat but with the presence of the chicken, and especially her third leg, infected with some disease from foreign parts. Molcho stood next to him opposite the cage and stared at the spectacle, fascinated and perhaps a little frightened too. The boy knew that his father would not have come to stand among these people and stare at a chicken with three legs, and he missed him very much. And although no one had ever condemned such spectacles to him, he knew that they were wrong. The anxiety that had been in him before he entered the café and had drawn him to the spectacle and the company of these people and the friendship of Molcho now brought ominous pictures before his eyes. Every now and then the corners of Molcho's lips twitched in a smile, as if he were seeing things in a dream. And the boy pretended to be very amused and tried to look closely at the chicken, who was hopping from side to side of her little cage, as if she were fighting some hidden enemy, and he was ashamed of his ignorance of the secret which would have enabled him too to enjoy and admire the spectacle. He waited impatiently for the time he had paid for to be up so that he could leave. During those moments he felt such a sense of desolation that he thought it would never leave him.

The sound of a quarrel broke out at the entrance to the café, where the quilt and mattress renovator could be seen trying to force his way in past the two men sitting by the money box, who were pushing him back and hitting him. Yardeni looked anxiously at the door, wondering whether to leave his post by the cage and to go investigate the reasons for the fight and restore order, or to let it alone and guard the chicken.

The quilt and mattress renovator shouted something from the doorway to the people inside the café, and the people asked one another: What's he shouting there, what does he want? —With carpenter's glue, he says, they stuck the leg on with carpenter's glue.

The alarmed Yardeni was driven to take a few steps forward again, in order to have a few words with the two men, but before he could reach the doorway he had to return to his post by the cage to guard it and restore order in the café, where the outcry was growing louder by the minute; and there was no knowing if the outcry was due to excitement and high spirits or to indignation at the fraud, or whether the people's frenzy was simply seeking a pretext for erupting after it had been inflamed by the sight of the freakish, contemptible chicken: in any case, the heavy cart driver with the sweaty cap brushed Yardeni out of his way, lifted the cage into the air with both his hands, hit the flimsy wooden slats with his fist and shattered it with a couple of blows. He removed the chicken, brushed aside her tail, and inspected her third leg. All the people crowded round and the chicken flapped her wings and squawked in pain as the cart driver attempted to tear the third leg out of her flesh. Again and again he tried to part the leg from the flesh of her body, pulling harder and harder as Yardeni entreated him: Have pity on dumb animals!

And suddenly they all saw the leg lying on the palm of the cart driver's hand and drops of blood falling from the chicken's white feathers. The people in the café burst into angry cries and laughter and they all rushed to the doorway to see the two men in all their guilt. But their places next to the table were empty, and the money box was gone too.

The cart driver dropped the chicken and threw the third leg in disgust at Yardeni, who recoiled in horror. Although drops of blood were still falling from underneath its tail, the chicken ran frantically about the café looking for the door, but she could not find it for the people filled the room and hid the light from her.

And when she bumped into the legs of the people who recoiled from her in disgust, because they had not forgotten her third leg, she flapped her wings and tried to fly away, as if she were a bird. Only the drunk, who was in a very quiet and thoughtful mood all this time, smiled at the panic-stricken chicken, held up an admonitory finger, and repeated: Vanity of vanities, vanity of vanities.

They stuck it on with glue, with glue, said Yardeni and clapped his hands despairingly, remembering the two men who had escaped with the money and left him with the chicken and the uproar in his café. The crowd began to leave. When they were outside Molcho said to the boy: You want to come and swing now or some other time? —Some other time, said the boy. —What a chicken, sighed Molcho, remembering with emotion the impact of the experience. —They stuck it on with glue, with glue. It's a shame my brother didn't see it. And once again he stretched out his hand to clasp the boy's shoulder, as a gesture of friendship. But the boy evaded him. Molcho went on his way without another word, and the boy knew that next time he encountered him Molcho would try to hit him again, as he always did, but he no longer cared.

When the boy reached home he stood outside the gate for a minute looking at the windows. Then he climbed the steps and the front door was locked. No one answered his knocking. He walked around the house and everything was shut up tight. He went into the back yard and saw the Arab sitting on the steps of the cowshed, without his fiddle, his head on his hands and his eyes staring vacantly.

In the afternoon Bruria's parents left the house and walked with her to the bus station. Bruria was quiet all the way, but when she saw the bus she shrank back and promised that she would be good. But her parents paid no attention to her promises. She wept silently and her mother too wiped a tear from her eye. But her father said: Let this be a lesson to you for next time, let this be a lesson to you.

I don't want the shoes anymore, said Bruria, I'm sorry. They got on the bus and Bruria covered her face with her hands and cried without stopping. Her mother, who sat beside her, embraced her and put her head on her shoulder, and her father, who sat in front of them, pretended not to know them.

The boy circled the house again, to see if anyone had come back in the meantime, but the doors and windows were all shut, and there was no one to be seen. He returned to the back yard and sat down opposite the big tap. He held the stem and wondered if the same thing that had happened before would happen again, but everything stayed the same and the afternoon hours stretched out endlessly.

In one of the deserted fields behind the citrus groves, outside the town, the quilt and mattress renovator lay on the ground with his eyes open, staring at the sky. A column of ants crawled over his arm and climbed up to his neck and down to the ground again, as if he too was part of the earth, a hump on its back.

It was a dreary summer afternoon and everything was empty and too quiet. The Arab rose lazily to his feet and went into the cowshed and started raking the manure into the gutters and from the gutters outside. The raking sounded like a scratching in the heart of the darkness. A slow drag of the rake, then a short silence, then a drag of the rake, then silence again. And the boy looked around him and waited for the thing to happen again, and he was seized with rage at the indifferent touch of the big tap, and affronted at being left alone. He said softly: I, I, I, I—and the magic did not work.

And suddenly his body was lifted sky-high in a familiar, well-beloved movement, and immediately he felt his father's face with its prickly stubble against his cheek. And the boy could find nothing to say to his father for shame filled him with a kind of fog. But he was afraid that his eyes would fill with tears and betray him if he did not open his mouth and say something, and so he whispered into his ear: Our grandfather is dead, our grandfather is dead. And his father hugged him and said nothing in reply, but carried him to the house and put him down next to the door and took him by the hand. Together they entered the house and his father led him into the big room and there was a secret smile on his face. They went into the big room and the boy looked around him and saw that nothing had changed and the room was the same as always. As if no one had ever lain there on the floor, and there had never been candles or anything. And the colors of the windowpanes as always cast purple, green and orange stains on the walls and tiles. And the boy did not understand what was before his eyes or the contradictions rising in his memory. He looked questioningly at his father, and then again at the room, and afterward he smiled at his father as if to ask: Did it really happen? And his father smiled back at him as if to say: Indeed it did.

Henrik's Secret

✽

translated from the hebrew by dalya bilu

How long is he going to go on being bad friends with me?"—Henrik's hoarse voice, which had sounded at first like an old woman's until I got used to it and it no longer jarred on my ears, except when it was being so serious and direct.

"Maybe until the end of the vacation"—a short, circumspect pause for deliberation—"and maybe later; I haven't decided."

We are both collecting shrapnel among the rocks on the mountainside and Henrik suddenly gets to his feet, stands up straight, raises his eyes for some reason to the midday sun, and twitches his nose like a rabbit, as if to straighten his thick glasses and bring the lenses closer to his eyes. He spreads his hands out sideways, like a tightrope walker trying to keep his balance—or more accurately, like someone caught in a bog, with every superfluous movement liable to make him stumble and fall. The skin on his face and body is always pink, a sickly pink, like skin which has been excessively scratched or burned, and his very fair yellow hair is straight as fine threads; and as he stands thus opposite the sun he looks to me like a photograph film my father once showed me, the negative of a child.

"It's gone on too long. It's time to end it. And he hasn't even told me what made him bad friends with me in the first place."

As he says this the yellow clown from the negative suddenly looks to me like an adult rebuking me, not angrily but patiently, with a bewildered and forgiving expression. Two voices speak in him, both of them hoarse, broken, rolling the r's and stressing the penultimate sylable in a foreign way, but one of them is mischeivous, reckless and eager, and the second is mature and somewhat remote. I don't say anything in reply but go on walking slowly and stooped over, searching for the shrapnel. He stands his ground, a new spirit has possessed him and he is not about to miss the opportunity:

"I want him to tell me right now what made him bad friends with me in the first place. What harm did I do him? Let him tell me one bad thing I did to him!"

From the little neighborhood on the top of the mountain—small stone houses, most of them one story and a few two stories high—the bay looks like a toy model, as if you could stretch out your hand and touch it: the blue sea, the ships entering and leaving the port, uttering long, deep growls that make them sound like prehistoric animals, the tiny cars driving on the roads past the suburbs and the two "yogurt jars" of the oil refineries, belching a thin, whitish smoke. And in the mornings the mountainside is strewn with fragments of shells and nobody can tell me when they fell here.

I remembered the reason why I was bad friends with him vividly, but I didn't want to remind him. It wasn't that I bore a grudge against him, but the decision to start speaking in the second person again would be painful because the reason for my hostility had become so obsolete, while the smooth, natural transition to the third person had been full of genuine feeling.

A few weeks before this, on a Saturday morning, his father had come to our house to ask my mother's permission to invite me over to their house, in order to meet Henrik and make friends with him. There were no other children of our age in that group of houses on our street, and accordingly my mother was glad of the opportunity, especially since Henrik's father made such a good impression on her with his fine manners and in the way he wanted to introduce us to each other.

The same day, after the afternoon siesta—wearing my best clothes, clean and combed—I went to the house behind the grocery store, to Henrik's house.

His father opened the door and shook my hand. He led me into the room and I saw the yellow-haired, pink-skinned, bespectacled child sitting at the table next to the chessboard. Opposite him was an empty chair, upon which his father had apparently been sitting and playing chess with him until my arrival. Henrik stood up, and when his father introduced me to him, he held out his hand and we shook hands like adults. Henrik was already sufficiently familiar with local mores to turn the handshake into a little performance, and he added a bow and prolonged it longer than usual even between adults, and when he released my hand he gave me a smile of complicity. He returned to the table, with one sweep of his hand felled all the chessmen which had been set out on the board, and in a surprisingly hoarse voice asked me if I knew the game. I shook my head. "Not draughts either?" he asked in a disappointed tone. I shook my head again.

Henrik's sister entered the room and Henrik called her and introduced her to me: Wanda. Again the handshake, but this time perfunctory, over in a second. She was much older, a young woman wearing a long, brightly colored dressing gown. Wanda gave me a very friendly smile and immediately returned to the room from which she had come (apparently the kitchen), where I heard her talking in their foreign language. A minute later she emerged and placed a little dish of sweets on the table and Henrik and I sat down.

From the same door Henrik's mother now entered the room. She was a silver-haired woman who looked more like his grandmother than his mother. She looked around her with dull and slightly panic-stricken eyes, examining the room as if she had landed there by accident and had never been there before in her life, and then she began walking slowly toward me, as if she were afraid of startling me if she approached too quickly. She stood opposite me, focused her eyes on my face, and said something to me in their language. Henrik burst out laughing and when I asked him what she had said he explained that his mother wondered what my parents said about the present state of the war.

He was laughing at his mother. This did not seem to shock his father—a thin, balding man, who placed his hands on the table and looked at his fingers—or for that matter, his sister, who stood in the doorway of the other room and surveyed the scene with total detachment. I imagined that they thought nothing of it, or that Henrik was allowed to do as he pleased at home.

On those summer evenings, when the blackout blocked the windows and a stifling heat filled the house, my father would sit with me and show me the different countries and the movements of the armies on the maps of the *Pears Encyclopedia*. But I saw only the shape of the Italian boot and the English dog standing on its hind legs and the French block balancing miraculously on the tip of Spanish block and our own Mediterranean Sea and Palestine, and sometimes I would copy these shapes with carbon paper onto a clean sheet. Sometimes I would make a mistake and put the carbon paper the wrong way up, and when I turned the page I would discover my drawings on top of the other maps. Gradually the whole *Pears Encyclopedia* atlas filled up with my drawings and my father looked at the scribbled pages and clapped his hands in helpless amusement and said that on our maps the borders had moved and the countries changed and the whole world was a muddle. Only my mother would sigh bitterly, and even though she assured me that it wasn't because of the spoiled maps, I couldn't think of any other reason for her to sigh. In days to come the distant war would appear to me in the form of the scribbled pages in the *Pears Encyclopedia* atlas and the shapes of the countries which had been ruined beyond repair.

Henrik said something in reply to his mother and made a gesture with his hand as if to send her away. Henrik's sister offered me a sweet, and I recalled my mother's instructions not to take anything they offered me because they were refugees and very poor. Their poverty, but expecially their displacement, impressed me deeply, and without understanding at all what the nature of this condition was, I knew in my bones that although they resembled our sweets in every respect, their sweets were not to my taste—like the smell in their closed room, as if it came from moldy clothes or the body of a mysterious animal which had been hidden somewhere.

Accordingly, I refused to take a sweet, and although Henrik's sister urged me repeatedly to do so I could not overcome my revulsion. Again I saw Henrik's mother coming toward me as slowly as if she were covering half a kilometer with every step she took. She held both hands out in front of her, and when she reached me she took my head in her arms and began rocking me as if she wanted to put me to sleep, grunting in their language as she did so. When I succeeded in extricating myself from her embrace I saw that she was crying. Henrik's father took hold of her arm and pulled her back to the door through which she had entered the room. I asked Henrik what his mother had said to me this time, but he didn't answer and laughed again, in enjoyment and without embarrassment.

His sister held out a sweet to me and I had no choice but to take it. I put the sweet in my mouth and sucked it without enjoyment. Henrik's mother came into the room again holding a tray with four cups of tea on it. The cups were very thin and had a pattern of pink and purple roses, as did the saucers upon which they stood. Henrik, apparently fearing another attempt by his mother to embrace me, hurried up to her and took the tray. His mother let him take it, without worrying that he might drop something or do damage, and Henrik took her by the elbow and guided her to a seat at the corner of the table, where his father and sister joined us. He placed the tray on the table and his sister set each person's teacup in front of him.

Henrik's parents spoke to each other in their language, and every now and then Henrik or his sister Wanda said something to them. Henrik's father turned to me and asked me about the school which I attended and which Henrik was to begin attending after the long vacation, but it was clear from his questions that it was not the school which interested him so much as my personal scholastic attainments, as if he were afraid I might have a bad influence on his son, or perhaps he was only trying to make conversation, so that I wouldn't sit in silence while they discussed their own affairs in their language.

After tea Henrik's father said: "Why don't you go outside to ride the bicycle?" He took a key out of the drawer of a small, dark table standing under the closed window, and gave it to Henrik. Then he accompanied us to the door and before he closed it he smiled at me as if to say: You'll see in a minute that you won't lose by the agreement between us.

We went out into the yard behind the grocery store where Henrik's bicycle stood—shining like new, and fastened, for some reason, with a lock. Henrik opened the lock and put it away in his trouser pocket, pushed the bicycle into the street and offered it to me to ride.

I didn't know how to ride a bicycle, but I had no intention of admitting this to Henrik. Instead, I muttered something or other, and rejected his bicycle with disgust. Neither of us said a word. Henrik put his right foot on the pedal and gave a big push forward with his left. Then he sprang onto the seat and began rapidly turning the pedals. He receded and disappeared round the bend in the road, and for a moment I thought that he wasn't going to come back to the place where I was waiting for him. But the next minute I saw him returning, leaning right and left, and making the bicycle tilt and swerve in broad, dangerous curves all over the road. Then he straightened up, turned around, took his hands off the handle-bars and rode past me waving his hands proudly in the air. His pale yellow hair, very fair and straight as fine threads, waved in the wind and glittered with his glasses in the sun, adding color to his tricks, and he uttered a gleeful cry in his hoarse voice, perhaps the kind of cry uttered by savages in the jungle. In the end he came flying down the street, turned round quickly and stopped abruptly, right at my feet, with his wheels screeching and kicking up sand at the sides of the road. His permanently scalded pink face smiled at me with satisfaction.

I looked at him dismissively, with a smile that was almost contemptuous, and went to sit on a stone at the side of the road. He leaned his bicycle against the fence and came to sit down beside me.

"Don't you know how to talk?" asked Henrik with adult sarcasm.

"I can't stand show-offs," I said.

"I'm not a show-off," protested Henrik. "We were in Tel Aviv for a bit and I didn't have any friends there. Now we're here and I still haven't got any friends. And when I'm alone, I haven't got anything to do. Either I play chess with my father, or I ride my bike and learn all kinds of tricks."

I wanted him to know that I hadn't lived in this neighborhood all my life either, but that we had come here from my town due to my father's work in the army. I told him about my home town and exaggerated its wonders—or perhaps that was how it really seemed to me in those days, when I was so far away from it. Two or three times a year we would go home for a visit. Once we traveled down by train and when we entered the corridor and stepped into the compartment we had to pick our way through dozens of Horanis, who were different from the Arabs I had known up to then, sitting on the floor in their rags with thousands of flies covering them and buzzing around them like a living black curtain, spotting their faces and sticking to their sick, festering eyes, and there was an appalling stench in the air, the stench of filth and bad sweat. There was a strange look on my mother's face, and I didn't know if she was going to burst into tears or laughter, and my father said that this was the last time we were going to travel by train.

After that we took the bus. On one of these trips there was a big man with a tattered peaked cap and a wild red beard sitting at the back of the bus, and all the way he never stopped crying and yelling: "Everyone fucks and I want to fuck too! I deserve a fuck too! There are blondes and brunettes, thin girls and fat girls, tall girls and short girls, refined girls and girls who wear ties and trousers too. And I haven't got a single girl to fuck. Everybody fucks and I want to fuck too! I've got the right to a fuck too!" He hardly changed the formula and repeated it over and over again. The passengers laughed or hid their faces in shame, or put on stiff, denying expressions (like my parents, for instance). The driver said that the man had got onto the bus in Safad and he didn't know what to do with him. I asked my father what the man was saying and my father replied: "You can see for yourself, he's a crazy drunk."

"But what does he want?" I persevered.

My mother came to his aid: "He wants nonsense! He's not normal, that's what he is."

She hoped that this would be the end of it—that I would stop asking questions, or he would stop yelling. But the man didn't stop and I looked at him in horror and fascination. "Everybody fucks girls and I want to fuck too! I've got the right to a fuck too!" My parents demanded that I stop looking at him. They explained that it wasn't nice and that I would offend him if he saw me staring at him and he might even lose his temper and since he was a crazy drunk there was no knowing how he might react. The terror bubbled inside me like huge laughter suppressed and stifled and my mother whispered to my father, who was sitting in the seat in front of us, that she really didn't know if traveling by bus was any better than traveling by train with the Horanis.

The man finally got off at one of the stations in the Sharon Valley. The sound of his crying went on echoing in my ears for many years to come, and whenever we got on the bus to travel to our home town, usually for Passover or the New Year, I would search the passengers for the man with the tattered peaked cap and the wild red beard, whom I never saw again. But to this very day, even as I write these words, if I concentrate for a moment I can clearly hear his voice sawing the air a few meters behind my right shoulder, exactly as I heard it then on the bus, when he was traveling from Safad to somewhere in the Sharon Valley, breaking into its bitter and piteous complaint, like a ham actor who'll use every trick in the book to win the hearts of his audience, and the harder he tries to win them the more disgusted they become.

I told Henrik that after the war we would return to our town, and that maybe that would be soon. Henrik laughed; he must have been better informed about the war situation than I was. We went back to their yard and Henrik put his bicycle in its place, took the lock and key out of his pocket, and locked it. I told him about the shrapnel you could find on the mountain. He couldn't understand where the shrapnel came from when there were no shells falling in the vicinity. I was hard-pressed to explain it to him, and to this day I don't know the reason myself. But he wouldn't leave it alone, the question bothered him. In any event, we went out to the mountain to search. When Henrik found his first piece of shrapnel, he examined it with great concentration, transferring the jagged fragment of iron from hand to hand and feeling its saw-like teeth with his fingers, as if trying in this way to discover how it had arrived here. Then he shrugged his shoulders and went to look for more fragments.

When evening fell the windows of the houses were blacked out and the street was in darkness. Only in the sky two searchlights wandered to and fro, lingering for a moment at some point high above and continuing their wanderings and disappearing for a while and reappearing again. Henrik looked into the sky and said: "They've invented some kind of special balloon against airplanes now. You can't see them in the dark, and when a plane collides with them it gets tangled up and explodes and crashes to the ground. I'm sure that the sky is full of those balloons right now."

I looked up and tried to see Henrik's balloons. For a moment it seemed to me that I could actually see circles floating like air-bubbles in the dark sky, but they vanished immediately. I looked at Henrik and he gazed in the direction of the dark sea at the foot of the mountain, the sea which had already merged into the sky for the duration of the night, and said: "And in the bay they've built chimneys that start smoking whenever an airplane arrives, and they cover the whole bay and all the surrounding area with smoke so that their planes can't see anything and they drop their bombs into the sea."

"My father works in the army and he didn't tell me about it," I said to Henrik.

"Maybe your father doesn't know," Henrik replied simply, as if this was very possible and perhaps even self-evident, and I kept quiet and stopped believing him. The business of the balloons too now seemed questionable to me. And in almost the same breath as he had said what he said about my father, he went on to ask: "And what are we going to do with all this shrapnel?"

When I failed to come up with an answer to his question, he raised his eyebrows and looked at the shrapnel as if it were nothing but rough, jagged pieces of scrap iron of no use to anyone.

"You collect it," I said.

"Would you like us to collect it together?"

"That's impossible," I said. "I've been collecting for ages and I've got tons of it, and you're just starting and you haven't got any so how can we be partners?"

And Henrik held out the pieces of shrapnel he had just collected and said: "So you take them. I've got nothing to do with them."

Before we parted to go home Henrik said: "Come to my house tomorrow too. We'll go and look for shrapnel."

"But not in the afternoon," I announced proudly, "because on Sunday my father doesn't work and we go for a walk in town and have 'five-o'clock' in the Café Panorama."

The next morning, when I went out into the street, Henrik was already riding up and down on his bicycle and demonstrating all his strange tricks again. And when he saw me he offered in all simplicity to teach me to ride the bicycle.

"I know how to, I just don't want to," I said.

"Never mind," said Henrik ingenuously, "get up and I'll hold the back."

The idea appealed to me and I swallowed my pride.

I sat on the bicycle and Henrik held the back. He showed me how to put my feet on the pedals and grip the handlebars firmly, and he began to run behind me, balancing the bicycle. I rode like this for a few yards, until I heard Henrik's hoarse voice asking behind my back: "Should I let go?" and I answered: "Yes, let go," and before the words were out of my mouth I was already lying on the road with Henrik's bicycle underneath me.

Henrik came running up behind me, picked me up and examined me to see if I was hurt. I stole a glance at the bicycle and saw that the mudguard of the back wheel was bent. When I saw this, I held my grazed knee in my hands and narrowed my eyes in pain, spat on two fingers and cleaned the blood and grit from the graze. Henrik bent down and examined the graze. "It's nothing, really," he said rolling the r in his irritating way.

"Nothing!" I cried and my hatred blazed. "Nothing! You did it on purpose! You pushed the bike sideways on purpose to make me fall, to make me break my head and legs, so I wouldn't be able to go to Café Panorama for 'five-o'clock' this afternoon!"

"That's not true!" protested Henrik, looking a little scared. "That's not true, I don't do things like that."

He twitched his nose nervously like a rabbit to bring the lenses of his glasses closer to his eyes. "Why should I make you fall, you're my friend!" He picked up his bicycle and he didn't look at the bent mudguard.

"I'm not your friend and I don't want to talk to you!" I said and walked home with a very pronounced limp. I didn't look back to see Henrik's reaction to my announcement, but I knew that he was standing in the street with his bicycle and looking at me, as I walked away with an affected limp and he was left alone again, as he had been in Tel Aviv, as he had always been.

In the afternoon I was dressed up in my best clothes and set out with my mother and father to go for a walk in town and take five-o'clock tea in the Café Panorama.

First we took the bus down to the lower town and went for a stroll in Kings Street, as was our custom when we went out on Sunday afternoons. We saw the Arab gentlemen in their black suits and ties, and my mother sighed in amazement as she always did and asked how they could dress like that in the summer heat. And with the gentlemen, or a little behind them, came the ladies wrapped in flimsy black veils, to protect their white faces from the ravages of the sun—or so my mother explained; and men in fezes rolling amber beads between their fingers behind their backs; and *fallaheen* in wide gathered trousers, and their women carrying heavy loads on their heads; and army officers passed before us in their uniforms, and government officials in their white pith helmets and tropical outfits. And sometimes my father would meet people from work, an English soldier or Arab clerk, and he would introduce my mother and me to them. And one of the soldiers we met bent down and asked me something in English, and my father whispered in my ear: "Say: 'George'." I mumbled something that was neither "George" nor anything else and panic seized hold of me because I didn't understand the question I had been asked or the meaning of the answer. I felt as if my father's well-being depended on my giving the correct answer and the word stuck in my throat and refused to come out. Again my father whispered in my ear, this time with a hint of impatience —Say 'George'; say 'George'—and I shrugged my shoulders and looked at my mother and father alternately and said nothing. The soldier stood up and exchanged a few more remarks with my parents, and I was forgotten. But the word "George" which had stuck in my throat would not let me be. I made another effort to pronounce it, even though the soldier and my parents were already shaking hands, but the word refused to emerge.

"Why didn't you say 'George'?" asked my father after the soldier was gone.

I kept quiet, very ashamed and agitated. And my father explained to me that the soldier had been testing me to see if I knew the name of the king.

On a pedestal in the middle of the junction, opposite the port, stood a policeman in spotless white sleeves and short trousers directing the traffic. Not far from there stood the bus which climbed the mountain and stopped at the Café Panorama.

From some distance away we heard the playing of the band, and my mother exclaimed happily: "Listen to that, they're playing all the hits already!" And she joined in and hummed the tunes. When we entered the café garden I immediately ran, as usual, to the bandstand, to see the musicians from close up, until my mother and father called me to come to the table and partake of whatever they had ordered for me. My parents stood up to dance and I hurried back to my corner next to the bandstand. When the artistic program began, the dancers returned to their seats.

The whistler Clara Imas whistled passages of light classical music and the audience applauded her with loud cheers. She trilled in tremulo, imitated bird calls and concluded with a Hungarian *czardas*, imitating the sobbing of a Gypsy violin. After her came the actor Michael Gore, who sang a few popular songs and then did his favorite turn: from his jacket pocket he took a little black comb and combed his hair onto his forehead, until it almost covered his eyes, and laid the edge of the black comb like a mustache on his upper lip, with the result that he looked just like Hitler, an effect which could also be produced by correctly folding the piece of paper with the drawings of four pigs on it obtainable for half a piastre at kiosks. The actor imitated Hitler's screams and lunatic speeches and the audience responded with peals of laughter and enthusiastic applause.

The band broke into dance music again and I looked at the people seated in the café garden and suddenly I saw Henrik's sister sitting at one of the more distant tables. I told my mother, and she pointed her out to my father. They both looked at her. My mother told my father about Henrik's father, who had visited our home and invited me to be his son's friend. My parents looked at Henrik's sister for a minute and marveled at her beauty.

"What's her name?" my mother asked me.

"Wanda," I said.

"Beautiful Wanda," said my mother. "How beautiful she is."

My father agreed with her and they both smiled at each other for a moment as if they were sharing a secret.

The low, round platform was next mounted by the singer Yosef Goland, sporting a fez on his head and two curly earlocks dangling from his ears, who began to sing a song I liked about "Saadia the Yemenite Shoe-Shine Boy." But I paid no attention to the song, I was too busy looking at the beautiful Wanda, who was sitting at a table at the edge of the garden with her legs crossed, and there was no knowing if she had come by herself or if the person she had come with had left her for a moment. The singer finished his song and began another, and I went on staring at the beautiful Wanda, Henrik's sister.

Her being so beautiful disturbed me. The fact of her beauty was axiomatic, since my parents had said so. If my father and mother told me that a person or an object or a landscape was beautiful I accepted it as gospel. I would simply try to examine the radiation of this beauty from the person or object or landscape in question, in order to adapt myself to the incontrovertible judgement pronounced by my parents. I would try to sense the essence of its beauty, how it was expressed, how it could be distinguished, to identify the signs that might enable me to recognize it for myself one day in the future; in other words, to guess in advance what my parents' judgement would be even when they were not by my side. I therefore examined Wanda's face and tried to explain to myself the secret of its beauty, to elucidate what set it apart from other faces, and what it was that made it so beautiful.

The singer concluded his performance, the band played dance music again, and my father and mother got up to dance. This time I didn't go to stand next to the band, but remained seated in my place, studying Wanda's face.

Wanda's hair was brown and curly, and her face was slender. Unlike her brother, her complexion was rather dark. Her chin was pointed, her lips narrow and coated with lipstick, and her two narrow, arched black eyebrows emphasized her big, dark, shining eyes. I said to myself that it was Wanda's eyes, especially her eyes, which were the signs of her beauty, their unusual shine and dark lashes, which cast a kind of shadow over her face when she looked down at the table. And also her abundant, curly hair and the earrings glittering in her earlobes, which made a kind of frame for her eyes. I tried to explain to myself the beauty of her mouth too, since it was clear that it was beautiful, like everything else about Wanda, but nevertheless it caused me a certain uneasiness, gave rise to a muffled anxiety for which I was unable to account: the narrow lips painted bright red and the narrow pointed chin. The taste of the sweet I had not wanted rose to my palate together with the smell of the closed room, a smell of moldy clothes or the body of a strange animal kept hidden there. Tirelessly I invented excuses and justifications, but for some reason it seemed to me that Wanda's mouth and chin belonged to somebody else's face, and threatened the perfect beauty of her real face, which was concealed behind them. Consequently they also prevented me from finding the full explanation for my parents' verdict and feeling confident that I had absorbed it properly.

Until it suddenly dawned on me that these lips and this pointed chin were Henrik's lips and chin which had invaded her face in order to falsify its beauty, and the memory of the morning and my fall from his bicycle came back to me after I had forgotten them completely. And when I focused my attention on Wanda's face to examine its beauty again, its order had been upset and I had to begin from the beginning: the hair, the eyebrows, the eyes, the earrings . . . to reorganize the whole composition and its justification. But I could no longer piece together the beauty which had been destroyed, reconstruct the secret which had been revealed to me for a moment and immediately lost. And suddenly our eyes met from the opposite ends of the café garden.

Wanda's eyes rested on me and I didn't know if her expression held the hint of a smile of greeting or surprise or apology or embarrassment. Perhaps it contained a mixture of them all. She raised her slender arched eyebrows and wrinkled her forehead slightly and the expression on her face grew clearer, concentrated into a single question: What do you want, little boy?

I felt this question directed at me and I couldn't answer it. Just as I couldn't say "George" when the English soldier asked me the name of the king, and my father whispered in my ear twice and implored me to say the word and save his honor in the eyes of the man from the place where he worked, and even urged me somewhat impatiently, and the word choked me and refused to come out. And now there wasn't even anyone to whisper in my ear and tell me the answer to the question on the face of the beautiful Wanda.

She picked up her handbag and put it down on the table, opened it and began searching for something inside it. For a moment she stopped searching and raised her eyes to me again, to see if I was still looking at her, as if the need to find whatever she was searching for depended on it. This second meeting of our eyes hurt me suddenly as if I were guilty of something I could not even imagine.

For a moment I attributed it to my quarrel with Henrik that morning, Henrik whose narrow lips and pointed chin had suddenly invaded his sister's beautiful face. But the pain was deeper, too mysterious to explain, it came from the area of things I wasn't yet supposed to understand, but whose acuteness I already felt, and whose danger was embodied in the damage I had done by upsetting the order of Wanda's beautiful face and disturbing her composure as she sat at the table on the edge of the café garden. As if I had broken some object I was forbidden to touch and the essence of the evil was not in the damage itself but in the transgression against a strict law which I did not know but was nevertheless commanded to keep.

I searched for my father and mother among the dancers on the floor and saw them laughing happily. Even though this relieved my anxiety about the possibility of their discovering my guilt, I felt, for the first time in my life, that they were no longer with me and would not be able to help me in my trouble, however they might wish to and try to and be obliged to. I brought my eyes back to Wanda searching in her handbag and worried about what she was looking for and whether it might harm me in some way. She looked in my direction again and once more our eyes met, but only for a split second, and now I felt alone and defenseless against her. She went on looking in her bag until she took out a little box, opened it, gazed into the inside of the lid (I knew it held a mirror, like my mother's) and examined her face. She took a powder-puff out of the box and applied it to her face. Then she looked into the mirror again, replaced the powder-puff, closed the box and returned it to her bag. With a certain hesitation she looked at the bag, raised her head, and again our eyes met. Suddenly her face grew grave and took on a decisive expression. She took a little coin-purse out of her bag, removed a few coins from it and placed them on the table. Then she returned the purse to the bag, shut the bag and rose to her feet. She lowered her eyes, examined her dress and straightened something, raised her head and walked out of the café garden.

The band took a break and my parents returned to our table.

They were in high spirits and when I informed them that Wanda had left they didn't understand at first what I was talking about, and when they did, they dismissed it with a shrug and went back to their chatting and laughing. I knew that I had indeed been abandoned, alone and destitute, to the plot in which I had become implicated by my own fault and that I had no one with whom to share this fate. I felt exceedingly glum, and when we got into the bus to go home my eyes filled with tears and my father who was sitting next to me hugged my shoulder and rested my head on his arm. My mother said: "He's tired," and I opened my mouth and said: "George, George, George, George, and his wife's name is Elizabeth, Elizabeth . . ." My parents burst out laughing, and I did not forget the memory of those hours of loneliness.

The next morning, when I went out into the street, Henrik was standing outside my house, without his bicycle, and he looked at me, waiting to see how I would behave. Since I had forgotten to limp, a hopeful expression crossed his face, but I remembered, albeit belatedly, and scowled at him.

"Where's his lousy bicycle?" I asked.

"At home," replied Henrik, without mentioning the bent mudguard.

"Does he want to go and look for shrapnel?" I asked.

"I haven't got any use for that shrapnel," said Henrik.

"But I need it," I said, "and he can collect it for me."

"What does he do with the shrapnel?" asked Henrik.

"I can't tell him," I said.

"I suppose it's something secret," said Henrik mockingly.

"Yes, it's secret."

And so we went down to the mountainside to look for shrapnel.

And suddenly, as we were bending down and searching the surface of the ground, Henrik straightened up in his characteristic way, raised his head to the sky, twitched his nose like a rabbit to bring his glasses closer to his eyes, and spread both arms out sideways as if to keep his balance.

"What a fool, what a fool I am!" said Henrik.

"What's the matter?" I asked.

"Now I understand, now I understand what my mistake was."

He kept quiet for a minute and looked at the sky, which apparently helped him to concentrate, and added: "Now I understand what I did wrong last night when I played with my father. If I hadn't made that mistake, he wouldn't have beaten me. I didn't think of it before."

He went to sit down on a rock not far from there, and I joined him and sat down beside him. And again he hit his temples with his fists as if to punish himself for his mistake and cried: "What a fool! What a fool!"

After that he was silent and I took one of the pieces of shrapnel which we had found and dug in the ground at my feet with it. In order to distract him from the business of his mistake, I told him about the man with the wild red beard who had shouted and cried in the bus: "Everybody fucks and and I want to get fucked too! I've got a right to fuck too!" Henrik looked at me and his eyes brightened and he no longer cared about the mistake he had made in the chess game with his father. Both of us sniggered for a long time and Henrik gazed far into the distance and the picture he saw there presumably afforded him great enjoyment. He rose from the rock and took up his previous position again.

"I know curses and terribly rude words that don't even exist in Hebrew," he said.

"Let him say them then," I requested.

And he spread out his arms and opened his mouth and with all his might he shouted at the sky the terrible words whose meaning I didn't understand, because they were said in their foreign language, but whose strange sound was enough to give me a frisson of illicit pleasure and a sense of licentiousness and filth. It was something like: *Pshchprkshzdjnshtrchdjkhoshch*.

It went on for a few minutes without stopping until Henrik's face grew red with exertion and enthusiasm and he lost his breath. In the silence which followed, the end of the harsh sounds and syllables went on reverberating for a moment in the air, sounds that held imprisoned within them a force which was very sinister and dangerous but which was also rousing and provocative.

Henrik looked at me with a triumphant smile and I did not suppress my admiration, or scorn his efforts, as I had done previously at the sight of his tricks on the bicycle. He resumed his seat on the rock beside me and we looked at the sea.

"Has he fixed his bicycle?" I asked. "The mudguard got bent when I fell."

"It's nothing," said Henrik. "I bent it back."

"Didn't they bawl him out at home because of it?"

"They didn't say anything."

"I want him to teach me those curses," I requested.

And he said them for me and repeated them syllable by syllable, and I tried to roll those wonderful sounds round my tongue and hiss them through my teeth, and Henrik burst into his hoarse, broken laugh with every mistake I made.

In the days that followed we would often sit on that rock, looking at the sea until evening fell, and teach my tongue to roll itself round those rude curse words, until I knew them all by heart and I no longer mispronounced them, even though I never attained Henrik's proficiency. But we still went on addressing each other in the third person, and Henrik never mentioned it, as if this was the normal way for people to speak to each other.

I know how full of shame the first moments of this transition to the second person will be. But why is it suddenly so important and urgent to him? In the face of my refusal his mood darkens and he demands in his serious voice, which reminds me of an old woman's voice, as on the day I first heard it, when I went to his house to become acquainted with him:

"I want him to tell me right now what made him become bad friends with me. What harm did I do him? Let him tell me one bad thing I did to him."

I don't know how to answer him. The afternoon lengthens and we don't speak. On our rock facing the sea we sit, Henrik resting his face on his hand. The pressure of his fingers on his face leaves white marks on his pink skin, which always looks irritated, as if suffering from a permanent burn. He sits in silence and I don't know what has suddenly gotten into him.

I commence the string of curses, and he stops me in the middle: "I won't speak to him at all, until he stops being bad friends with me. I won't answer him."

"But what does he care?" I shouted. "He's my best friend!"

"That's a laugh," said Henrik, "my best friend, my best friend, and that's how he talks to me."

We were silent again for a long time and I was afraid that Henrik would get up and go away and I would never see him again. This fear brought him closer to me than ever before. I was afraid that he wouldn't want to go with me to the Charlie Chaplin movies we had arranged to go and see together that evening in the community hall. And suddenly Henrik said:

"If he makes it up with me I'll tell him a secret that even my father and mother don't know."

This appealed to me as a possible way out. I agreed to the deal.

"I'll tell him after the movie," said Henrik.

At the appointed hour we walked to the community hall and sat down on one of the wooden benches to see the funny movies. We saw Charlie Chaplin waddling between the carriages standing on the railway tracks and policemen chasing him and him running away from them and hiding and getting up to various tricks, and everybody laughed, with Henrik's hoarse voice guffawing at my side the loudest of all. I tried to participate in his laughter, even though I couldn't understand what was going on in the movie or what was so funny about it. And Henrik slapped his knees and his head and laughed so much that he couldn't seem to find a place for himself on the bench. I contorted my face in laughter, but I knew that it wasn't enough. I was ashamed of being exposed to Henrik in my lack of understanding and I prayed for the movies to be over. I was hurt by Henrik's laughter, by the way he had suddenly forgotten his sorrow at my being bad friends with him and no longer cared at all. How quickly he had forgotten something which had made him so miserable only a couple of hours before. Now he was with himself and with Charlie Chaplin, and perhaps he had even forgotten that I was beside him and that he was supposed to tell me a secret after the movies were over. And perhaps it would no longer be worth his while to tell me his secret since in any case I didn't matter to him at all and it made no difference to him if I was bad friends with him or not.

The movies began to get on my nerves, and the more Henrik laughed and enjoyed himself, the more I hated the ugly little fellow waddling and skipping about with his cane and his rags, escaping from his pursuers who were even uglier than he was and whose faces were full of hair, and the sight of the black railway carriages and the greyish air all around and the murky light coming from the crooked lamppost at the edge of some junkyard—all these things together with the howls of laughter of the audience and of Henrik in particular reminded me, in the disgust they aroused in me, of the sight of the three-legged chicken exhibited in Yardeni's café in the town, a long time ago, on the day my grandfather died, and I remembered the audience standing round the cage, laughing and shouting provocatively at the monster.

At the end of the last movie we rose from the bench and Henrik's eyes were red from laughing and narrowed in the transition from darkness to the light which went on in the hall. I wondered if Henrik was still with me or if he was so far away now that he would think of nothing but Charlie Chaplin and his disgusting escapades and regret his promise about the secret.

I didn't ask him or try to remind him. When we came out of the hall next to the water tower he told me to wait and we both stood and waited. The audience dispersed and the street emptied and Henrik said: "He can come now." I followed him and I didn't know what all the ceremony was about.

We reached the entrance to the café and Henrik put his finger to his closed lips as a sign to me to keep quiet. We went into the dark, neglected, deserted garden in front of the café and heard sounds of music and dancing and peals of laughter coming from the building. We circled the wall of the café and reached the corner of one of the open windows, where Henrik crouched down and I followed suit. He signaled me to remain seated where I was, and he slowly straightened up, hugging the wall and the window frame, peeked inside and signaled me to stand up. I stood up and saw the interior of the café, festooned from wall to wall with colored lights that were dimmed on account of the blackout, and foggy with cigarette smoke, as if a fire had just been put out in the room. Drinking soldiers were sprawled on the chairs, and some of them were dancing with girls to the strains of a gramophone set upon one of the tables. Among the girls was the beautiful Wanda, locked in an embrace with one of the soldiers.

Henrik was riveted by the sight, and I too watched his sister Wanda, who was laughing incessantly and too loudly, wriggling her shoulders in an attempt to extricate herself from the soldier's clumsy embrace, but to no avail. Her luxuriant curly hair waved with the movements of the dance and sweat stained the armpits of her brightly colored dress. I didn't know how to connect this Wanda with the Wanda I had seen in the Café Panorama and with the Wanda my parents had said was so beautiful, nor did I know how to react to the spectacle before my eyes. I looked at Henrik. He seemed spellbound, and perhaps he had forgotten my presence at his side again.

The dance came to an end and someone got up to change the record on the gramophone, but the soldier didn't want to let Wanda go and she pushed him violently away. He swayed on his feet for a moment and fell to the floor. His friends burst out laughing loudly. Wanda sat down on one of the chairs, panting and fanning her flushed face with her hand, and as in the Café Panorama she opened her handbag and took out the little box, examined her face in the mirror and applied the powder-puff to her face. Henrik stayed rooted to the spot with his eyes fixed on his sister in a look full of love and tenderness and devotion.

I put my hand on his shoulder to tell him that I was there and also to tell him something else that I didn't know how to formulate, and he recoiled in alarm and looked at me as if I were a stranger. I had never seen him look like that—so serious, so grown-up and remote from me. I dropped my hand from his shoulder and he looked around, to make sure that nobody was coming to catch us. Again he looked inside and again he had the same expression of tenderness and devotion in his eyes as he watched his sister applying the powder-puff to her face. Together with her he turned his face to one side, and tilted his chin, as if he wanted to help her powder her face, like those mothers who make chewing motions with their mouths while feeding their babies, hoping that perhaps this will help them to swallow their food. Wanda put the little box back into her bag and stood up, and another soldier accompanied her to the counter. They received two drinks and stood there drinking, talking and laughing. Henrik went on participating in her facial expressions, smiling with her when she laughed and putting on an inquiring expression when she asked a question and waited for the soldier to answer her.

"Let's go," I urged him.

"In a minute," he said and went on looking.

"They'll catch us and break our necks."

He didn't answer me and kept his eyes fixed on his sister. I sat down under the window and waited until he finished looking and I was very bitter at heart because the promise had already been kept and there was nothing more to look forward to. After a few minutes he sat down next to me, saying nothing. And so we sat in silence opposite the hedge surrounding the cafe, leaning against the wall, darkness all around, while the window above our heads emitted a cloud of cigarette smoke, riding on the dim rays of light coming from the hall and on the strains of the dance music from the gramophone and the laughter of the soldiers and the girls.

Suddenly Henrik broke his silence and I heard him whispering the string of curses in his language between his teeth, but this time not in a yell of triumph and defiance against some hidden power, but with a certain apathy, skeptically, in the feeling that they were nothing but words, that they would change nothing. And when he finished the string, he repeated it again, in the same weak, disappointed tone, and when he finished the second time he got up and I followed suit and we moved along the wall at a crouch and crossed the dark garden and made for the water tower square.

Henrik walked without speaking and I walked next to him. I didn't know what to say to him. We walked down the dark, empty street and passed Henrik's house and then we passed my house and we went on and stepped off the road onto the mountainside and walked until we reached our rock. We sat down and there was silence between us.

After a long time I said: "Do you think that there are antiaircraft balloons in the sky now too?"

Henrik raised his eyes to the sky, contemplated it for a while, and said: "I think so."

"But you can't see them in the dark," I remarked.

"They made them like that on purpose, so that the airplanes wouldn't be able to see them."

"Maybe the sky is full of those balloons right now," I said.

"So full that they're touching each other."

The beams of two searchlights were wandering slowly over the sky, at the two ends of the invisible horizon, but even in their light we couldn't see the balloons.

It was late but neither of us got up to go home, even though we knew that our parents were looking for us.

Henrik rose thoughtfully to his feet.

"It wasn't any good today," he announced. "The other times it was much funnier."

And he began sniggering to himself.

But I couldn't join in his sniggers. From some hidden corner inside me, which knew Henrik's secret and had always shared it even before he revealed it to me, and even when he didn't take me to see the funnier things, there rose the picture which fascinated me and prevented me from behaving as I wished: Wanda laughing in the arms of the drunk soldier, more beautiful than she had ever been, far more beautiful that she had actually been in the café that night, fearfully beautiful, as I had at last learned to understand, moving very slowly as if in a swoon, in a dream, surrounded by colored lights and sweet tunes—and opposite her, Henrik looking through the window from outside, his eyes half-closed, abandoning himself longingly to the shape of her every movement, her every moment, as if he were trying to save her from some danger by putting himself in her place and transferring to himself the harm liable to be directed at her. And he too was not the boy I knew, for the danger challenging her enveloped him too in the atmosphere of dream-like beauty. He was not the boy standing opposite me at that moment on the dark mountain and laughing, putting his arm around my shoulders and crying in his hoarse, elderly voice: "What a laugh, what a laugh!" clapping his hands, slapping his knees and laughing without stopping, trying to shake me out of my trance, to tear me from the mesmerizing picture.

And when all his efforts to rouse me to laughter did not help, he too stopped laughing, moved a few steps backward and examined my face. We stood facing each other in silence, for a moment which seemed to last an hour, and suddenly he came up to me, raised his hand and slapped me hard in the face. "Why don't you laugh? Laugh! Go on, laugh!" yelled Henrik and went on slapping my face.

My cheeks burned. I turned on my heel and walked slowly back along the mountain path. I knew that he was still standing there and that he would soon follow me. I pressed my hands to my aching cheeks and when I stepped onto the road I felt more protected, even though I was surrounded by darkness and the houses revealed nothing of what was inside them.

After a minute I heard him dragging his sandals on the road, a few steps behind me, breathing heavily. When I reached my front gate I stopped to watch him walking past me. He reached the gate, and stopped in front of me, silent and panting. And in the darkness separating us from each other I couldn't even see through the lenses of his glasses.

Musical Moment

✳

translated from the hebrew by betsy rosenberg

The bird on the tray was gorgeous. With green and purple feathers, pampered and plump it sprawled heavily on the cold copper that sent its image back in broken reflection. The lanky neck drooped over the metal rim of the tray, looping through languor or self-love, head tucked, beak grazing the base of the bloody throat, the eyes glazed, stunned, despairing, pining over the catastrophe.

I never wearied of looking at that picture. Each Sabbath afternoon when we used to visit my father's Aunt Frieda, I would stare at it for a long while in a deliberate effort to learn the secret: why did the picture evoke in me a feeling of dangerous pleasure? Slightly to the right of the picture in the corner of the room sat my father's grandmother in her customary chair, a clean, wide, well-starched kerchief tied around her head in a triangle, the point touching her collar, the broad base overhanging her blind eyes, shading them. She sat in her armchair, there in the corner, like a stranger, an emissary from a world as yet unknown to me. Her face was doughy and her toothless mouth would gape from time to time as if to speak, then close abruptly with a compression of the lips and a look of resignation as though it would be too bothersome to say anything. Sometimes the glimmer of a smile would spread over her countenance only to fade among her countless wrinkles and finally vanish into the look of resignation.

We used to visit her each Sabbath afternoon. My father's Aunt Frieda opened the door for us, handsomely dressed as always, a chestnut wig curling down to her neck and two exquisitely dainty amber earrings hanging from her lobes. She was an elderly woman, but pretty nonetheless, elegant, tall and slender, and I will always recall her face reflecting goodness. Her husband, my father's uncle, stood by his old mother, shouting into her ear whenever someone arrived. Sometimes deafness impaired her wits or else memory failed her, and then my father's uncle would speak to her in their first language, identifying the relative who had just walked in, and she would nod to show she understood. Sometimes she would mutter something in her husky crone's voice and then her son would laugh uproariously, sporting with his old mother to entertain the company.

A light green cloth with shining gold fringe was laid on the round table, and next to it sat my two German "aunties," my father's cousins, Frieda's daughters. We could hear my father's uncle in hilarious conversation with his old mother about the coming of the Messiah or some such thing, until Frieda begged him to stop. Then she sliced and served the pale cake and we washed it down with a glass of thick, sweet wine.

My two German aunties were talking cheerfully in their language. Having settled their business, they gave me an appraising look and entered into conversation with my parents on the subject of my blinking. My parents hinted that they should drop the subject since I would be sure to understand what they were talking about, and my father pressed my shoulder to show me that he didn't care about my blinking. And my mother told them in their language not to mention it in front of me again because it would only upset me and aggravate the blinking. And when I heard her say that, I was surprised, because I didn't feel upset in the least, and I told myself that even my own mother didn't know my real feelings. And maybe no one ever would.

Erna, my father's cousin, was forceful, enterprising and stubborn, whereas her sister was reticent, a pacifier, inclined to mild depression. They were almost inseparable, though each sister had a family of her own. My parents' hints and appeals were of no avail. Erna ignored them. She believed with all her might in self-control and willpower. She rose from the table, took me by the hand, and told me to come along. My father grinned encouragingly to offer me support; no doubt, in anticipation of what I was in for with his cousin. She led me to the far side of the room, sank me down on the big, dark old leather couch, and sat beside me. She leaned over me, her face so close to mine I could see her pores and the faint quivering of her wrinkles. Behind Erna's shoulder I saw the old woman sitting in the corner, and above her, a little to the left, the picture of the expiring bird. First of all, Auntie Erna let me know, in her opinion the blinking business was due to pampering, like thumb-sucking among little children. And just as we fight thumb-sucking, we can fight this blinking too. The way to fight thumb-sucking, as we all know, is to sprinkle mustard or hot pepper on the offending finger, so that when next the child puts it in his mouth, the result is so disastrous that he will think twice about doing it again, unless, that is, he wants another taste of hell. And there are likewise devious strategies against blinking which for the moment she would not divulge. And lest I forget, the fight against blinking, like the fight against thumb-sucking, is waged for the sake of the child, the child and his family. Auntie Erna, pronouncing "family" in her special German accent, beamed with a look of surpassing responsibility and earnestness. We know of course, she said, that thumb-sucking is dangerous. There are juices in the mouth that decompose matter, so that the sucked thumb is gradually eaten away until nothing but a stub is left, which is so spindly that it falls off before you know it, and the child has a handicap for the rest of his life. As for blinking, we know that the lids are connected to the eyes with tiny muscles whose job it is to protect that most dear to us of all, our eyes, from dust and foreign matter. But if the muscles are abused, they deteriorate like a worn-out hinge that lets the door bang every time the wind blows, leaving the house open to havoc. Children who abuse their eye muscles lose control over them, so that sometimes while they're sleeping in the middle of the night they open their eyes without even noticing it, like certain kinds of animals. When this happens they have the most *horrid* nightmares.

"This must be stopped!" said my Auntie Erna. "It upsets your parents and embarrasses the entire 'family.' People ask questions, they don't understand. And if not for the sake of your own well-being and further development, then at least for the sake of the 'family' you must make every effort to stop this ugly, ugly blinking."

Pronouncing "ugly, ugly," Auntie Erna made a face, jerking, twisting it vehemently this way and that, squeezing her eyes shut, contorting her body, compressing her lips, then opening her eyes and goggling, then suddenly squeezing them shut again to show me just how terrible it looked. I knew she was overdoing it and I burst out laughing. Erna couldn't help laughing herself, but she kept saying, "That's how it looks! I want you to know that's exactly how it looks!"

My auntie, Erna's sister, approached the leather couch and asked her sister to leave me alone and come back to the table. She couldn't sit there without Erna. But Erna rattled away in their language and her sister smiled sadly, apologetically, and made a small gesture of dismissal and resignation. She remained standing near us for a little while longer and then went back to the table.

My Auntie Erna arrived at a new step-by-step procedure to stop my blinking. I was to count to twenty between blinks. After getting used to that, I was to count to thirty, and then forty. By the time I reached a hundred, she assured me, the habit would be broken. She asked me to begin, there and then, with the first exercise, from the simple to the difficult, to count to twenty without blinking. I did as she asked. Watching her, I began counting in a low voice. When I got to seven, I already had a strong impulse to close my eyes, if only for an instant, but I controlled myself.

Little by little the room grew dim around me, when all at once I noticed my father's old grandmother, facing me, sequestered in her chair. And through the dimness I thought I saw her clasping her hand over her head in a signal of distress. She was probably only adjusting her kerchief, but I perceived it otherwise, and I heard my Auntie Erna as though from far away counting with me in a loud, measured voice, nine, ten, eleven, a voice that chastened and commanded like a fateful clock, unrelenting, twelve, thirteen, fourteen . . . and my eyes were brimming over with the strain and I could no longer see my father's old grandmother because now my lashes were jammed together, tenaciously.

My parents rushed to deliver me from Erna who was sounding her disappointment and ridiculing me. My failure implied her own, the failure of her system and maybe even of the "family," and she raged at my parents for being too lenient and for spoiling me to my detriment. "He'll never stop," said my Auntie Erna. "He'll never stop. He won't even try, not for his own sake, not for his parents' sake, and not for the sake of the 'family.'"

My father wiped my eyes with his handkerchief and I kept trying to explain that I wasn't really crying, that the tears were falling because of the strain. But they wouldn't listen to what I said, either because they didn't believe me or because they didn't think it was important. But it was important to me. Because I had to vindicate myself so Erna wouldn't think I was a spoiled and inconsiderate crybaby. When I opened my eyes next I was back at the table facing my auntie, Erna's sister, who smiled her crushed and sorry smile. Erna herself was holding forth, and I knew they were talking about me. My father's Aunt Frieda returned to the table with an iridescent glass dish full of sweets. She set it down before me and stroked my neck. I wiped the last tears away with the back of my hand, and I hated my Auntie Erna for putting me to shame.

On our way home I asked my parents to please let me take up my violin lessons again. The lessons had been discontinued some years before against my will. I have never forgotten the aroma of colophony. It reminded me of separation and of the initial high hopes, a sour sort of bitter, heady smell. My imagination soared on it, and my heart thrilled with adventure. It seemed to pass from the rosined bow to the strings, from the strings to the sound, and into the very enigma of the violin, into its soul. On our way home I had a violent longing for it and for my violin, which had been taken from me for medical reasons.

Long consultations had been called for at the time. In those days, toward the end of the war, when we were living in a small neighborhood on Mount Carmel, I went with my mother to a two-story house on one of those quiet streets near the Institute of Technology, where I met my first violin teacher, Mrs. Chanina. She was tall and ample, with chestnut hair in a thick Russian-looking braid that rolled down her neck. My first violin teacher Mrs. Chanina tested my musical ability and consented to give me lessons. As my mother left the teacher's room she announced that my father would buy me a "quarter" violin and we would come for lessons twice a week.

This was around the time I first associated the alluring aroma of colophony with my teacher Mrs. Chanina. I saw in her a hitherto undreamed-of beauty and majesty. If today I saw her or a picture of her from those days, perhaps she wouldn't look so beautiful and majestic anymore. But I do understand what made her so exciting. It was the Slavic grace of her manner when she spoke. She had a deep, soft voice and eyes the color of her hair, the color of her drapes and furniture, brown with an auburn luster, a velvety brown with subtle, warm highlights. Her stature, her thoughtful, unhurried movements, her bearing, and her way of tilting her head a little to the right, all this raised her high in my esteem. And when she lifted her violin to play, her eyes flashed fire. As if the sleeping Gypsy were stirring in her, as if the violin were stirring her Gypsy blood to frenzied provocation, that's how I picture her today when I close my eyes and try to imagine her, the way she moved.

She was so friendly, too, she spoke so gently, and she held dominion over her surroundings like a queen. Around this time I had my first whiff of colophony, and I rubbed it assiduously on my bow. My father found "colophony" for me in the encyclopedia: so named after a small village in Asia Minor, whence this substance was exported. A clear yellow or light brown solid, it is derived from the residue of distilled turpentine. Nonsoluble in water, it will dissolve in ether or alcohol. Used in the manufacture of lacquer, to caulk boats, to rub on the bows of stringed instruments, and as a reducing agent in metal smelting; used predominantly in manufacture of soap and pharmaceuticals and as an emollient in the preparation of various salves and ointments.

Some time later, Mrs. Chanina observed that I had made excellent progress, and she suggested that my parents enroll me at the Haifa Conservatory to study theory. One winter afternoon my parents took me to the conservatory. They settled whatever they had to settle in the office, and led me to one of the classrooms. They were going to wait for me in the corridor. As I struggle to recapture these hazy, incoherent scenes, an abysmal feeling pours out of my heart to vent itself on the world. But I can't think why.

When I walked into the classroom with the secretary, the other pupils, who were older than I, were already seated and waiting for the lesson to begin, and they probably turned to look at me. I was to occupy a double desk next to a boy who had the beginnings of a mustache. He was leafing through his notebook, and I don't know what went through my mind just then, but I was probably nervous. I must have wondered what would happen now and what I was doing here among these older children who had nothing to do with me. And I imagined I heard wisecracks and giggling from some quarter, though it may not have been directed at me. A hush fell over the room as our teacher, a white-haired gentlemen with silver spectacles, walked through the classroom. He spoke to the class, and played something on the piano. Then he asked questions, and the pupils answered. We were on the top floor of the old building, and through the narrow window I could see the street below, the people, the traffic, the cyclists, the Arab vendors with their carts. Gradually the pallid winter sky gave way to dusk, and lights went on in the street and in the houses. Then the classroom lights went on and the faces of the older children were visible again, and the boy beside me was writing in his notebook. My notebook lay before me, blank and new. I couldn't think of anything to write. I thought about my parents waiting for me in the corridor, and I was impatient for the lesson to be over so we could go home.

Afterward my parents asked me eagerly about the lesson, and I said it was fine. Had I understood what they were learning? Yes, yes, I lied, I understood. They were very pleased with me and I couldn't look in their eyes. I knew I mustn't disillusion them. Their loving enthusiasm made this clear enough. I remember this as my first humiliating encounter with failure, and with the shame of having to lie to disguise it.

How comforting it was to be back with my teacher Mrs. Chanina, in the house I knew so well. I hoped I would never return to the conservatory, but a week later my mother took me again. I walked into the classroom and sat down. This time the chair next to mine was empty, the boy with the beginning of a mustache having moved elsewhere, to sit with one of the older children. I slid over to be near the window, where I could watch the traffic in the street and the people hurrying like swarming locusts. I don't know why, but suddenly I was seized with anguish. The whirling and swirling eddy of traffic made me so dizzy I might have fallen out the window and lost everything I had. I tried to turn my eyes away, but I couldn't. In the street one familiar figure stood out prominently against the crowd. She was looking directly at me, beckoning for me to jump down. I could see her clearly, her features, her gestures, and there was no mistake about it, she was addressing me. She opened her arms to embrace me. Then she vanished, and I finally managed to turn away from the window. The eerie scene had worn me out, and I was drowsy. I saw the older children writing in their notebooks as the teacher played various scales on the piano and commented in a weary, monotonous voice. I hid my face in my hands, wishing it would be over soon. I tried to visualize the corridor behind the door, to penetrate the wall, to make sure she was waiting for me. I tried to imagine myself pacing up and down the empty corridor with nowhere to go. I was getting as far as the office at the head of the stairs when a peal of laughter startled me, and as I dropped my hands I saw the entire class in an uproar and the old teacher leaning over to pat my shoulder. He smiled a little doubtfully, and another peal of laughter rang through the room.

Then he continued with the lesson. On my right was the dangerous window, and on the left, at the far side of the room, was the door that led to the corridor. I glanced around. I picked up my blank new notebook and tiptoed to the door. Slowly I turned the handle, opened the door, closed it stealthily behind me. Just as I had thought, my mother wasn't there. I walked down the empty corridor the way I had in my imagination, feeling abandoned and betrayed; I bit my lip, so I wouldn't scream. I stopped at every doorway and listened for my mother. Gradually my sense of propriety gave way to angry despair, and in furious pursuit, I opened door after door and peeked into each of the rooms, where I found lessons in progress, people quietly sitting about, or no one there at all. But my mother wasn't anywhere to be found. From the end of the corridor I heard a violin playing with piano accompaniment. I hadn't paid attention to it earlier because of my desperation. But as I approached the doorway, I heard the music clearly now, and it was sad and beautiful and mysterious. The door wasn't closed all the way and I peeped into the room, but I couldn't see anything. I opened the door a little wider and I saw the violinist, a tall boy wearing shorts and knee socks. His hair was black, combed neatly, and he was playing a large violin. He was so absorbed in the music that he closed his eyes; when his left wrist quivered over the bridge during the vibration, he bent over in his great emotion, and then he braced upright while playing the string passage. I could only see his profile, but the pianist was facing me, and she was a nice-looking girl with curly hair and glasses. They were alone in the room, absorbed in the music. Suddenly, the boy stopped playing and they talked, and I was afraid they would discover me behind the door, so I stepped back. Then they started from the beginning, and I resumed my post by the door and listened.

The music, sometimes lyrical and sometimes passionate, was touching me. My fear and pain and loneliness of a few minutes before were thrust aside before the sadness and the dignity, the surrender and the rebellion, the order and the flow of this beautiful music in three-quarter time. Sometimes the violin would draw out the theme, almost weeping, while the piano challenged and provoked, trying to break its line of thought, and sometimes the piano accompanied in conciliation, in joy or contrition, indulging the violin, cherishing, clinging. One variation gave way to another, and the piano sang the theme, true in its fashion to the sad, ennobling beauty of the melody, while the violin opposed it with a counter-rhythm, meeting the piano at the cadences, then leaving it again, until they finally merged.

When they had played through the final variation, the pianist stood up, and I stepped back and leaned ever so innocently against the wall. They left the room, she with her music tucked under her arm, he lovingly holding his violin case. They stood in the corridor talking together, and I longed to be him instead of me. I watched him from afar, my fear and self-pity giving way to a new emotion, that took me out of myself. The pianist said good-bye and walked into one of the rooms. He wandered down the corridor, aimlessly it seemed, lost in his reflections. Just then the pupils from my class began to pour out the door, and the boy with the beginning of a mustache called out "Uri!" and the violinist turned around, happy to greet him. The teacher came out of the room and looked at me as if he didn't know who I was, and then I saw my mother hurrying up the stairs.

"Were you waiting long?" she asked breathlessly.

"The class just got out," I said.

"How was it?"

"Fine."

"Did you participate?"

"Uh, no."

"Why not? Didn't you understand it?"

"I don't ever want to come back here again," I said, purse-lipped.

I refused to look at her, so I shall never know the expression on her face. She was silent. She held my hand and we walked down the stairs. I felt guilty with my hand in hers.

"I saw you down in the street, so I knew you weren't waiting for me." Now I could look at her. She bit her upper lip. "Is that why you don't ever want to come back?"

"No," I said, "that's not why."

Later, on the bus as we were winding up the hill, I told her about the boy and the wonderful music. She asked me to sing it for her and I sang what I thought sounded like the melody into her ear. It sounded pitiful to me compared to Uri's playing, but my mother was very impressed, and that evening when my father came home from work, she asked me to sing it for him. But however much I tried, it was lost, every note of it; all that was left was the memory of impression.

"Why don't you want to go to the conservatory anymore?" asked my father.

I didn't know what to say.

"Was it because I didn't stay and you were afraid of being alone?" asked my mother, with a trace of severity in her voice.

"No." I said. "Because it's not good there. They don't teach well."

"Why don't we give it some more time?" my father suggested, and I relented. My mother promised never to leave the corridor again when she was supposed to be waiting for me. I told my parents nothing at all about those lessons. Today, they seem like a strange dream that has neither beginning nor end. For years I have been trying to forget them.

Whenever I practiced the violin, Uri haunted me. My own playing seemed contemptible to me, no matter what my teacher Mrs. Chanina or my parents said. I despaired of attaining those magnificent heights, the domain of my betters.

One evening my mother asked me what was bothering me. I didn't know why she looked so worried. Did I sleep well, she wanted to know. When my father came home from work he too seemed worried. Strange, unaccountable things were going on, but they were outside, beyond my control, and there was nothing I could do about it. It concerned me, yet did not concern me. I was charged with a dark secret even I was not allowed to know, but which I had to keep until it could be told.

That winter and the following spring were unexceptional to all outward appearances, and yet, there was something in the atmosphere, something dark lurking around me, something that sneaked up on me and tried to sap my last reserves.

Twice a week my mother took me to the conservatory, and I would sit in the class like an outsider. No one ever paid attention to me, and I must have gotten used to it. I never heard a word they said. I only hoped to meet that boy Uri some day and ask him what the piece he played was called. But I never did meet him, and whenever I walked down the corridor with my mother I would pull her to the doorway where I'd heard him play, and beg her to wait and listen: maybe it would happen, maybe I would relive the fabulous moment. But usually no one was inside, or else someone else was playing in the room. It was the same with every other room along the dingy corridor. He had vanished.

One day before the lesson, the boy with the beginning of a mustache walked up to me and asked me why I blinked all the time. I was confused, but I realized he was a bully and trying to hurt my feelings. I didn't answer him. After the lesson I told my mother about the boy and what he had said. She looked so pained I was ashamed of myself. I felt as if I had the plague, or as if I were witnessing some terrible disaster, and I couldn't stop it, and no one could save me, and all they could do was confirm it or reassure me a little.

"If anyone asks you," said my mother, "just tell them you're tired. Say your eyes need rest. And after you rest it goes away. Just say you need rest. Rest is the best thing." The strain of telling a lie showed on her face. I wasn't tired. I didn't need to rest, and my eyes didn't either. And no one could give me what I needed. I looked at my face in the mirror. Nothing unusual there. It seemed like a conspiracy of silence.

"Are you feeling better?" asked the doctor. He was standing next to my father and mother as if they were all in league.

"Yes," I said, "I'm fine."

"Has anything unpleasant happened lately?"

I tried to think, but I couldn't remember anything of the kind.

He peered into my face but avoided looking at my eyes.

"How old are you?"

"Seven."

"Do you bite your nails?" He looked at my hands.

"What?! That's crazy!" I told him.

My mother shuddered, but I didn't know why. I searched her eyes, trembling at the prospect of disgrace. The doctor noticed my discomfiture and advised my parents to leave the room so he and I could have a little talk. When they were out of the room, he smiled at me and asked: "How are your parents, okay?"

"They're fine." I said.

He chuckled skeptically and asked, "Do they give you a hard time?"

"What do you mean?" I wondered. "What do you mean, they give me a hard time?" I loved them so much. What could he be thinking of?

"Do you think they're pleased with you?"

"I do whatever they tell me," I said.

His eyes lit up at this. He must have heard the undertone of anger in my voice.

"Are my questions making you angry?" asked the doctor.

"No," I protested. "No."

He smiled a dubious smile.

"Hey, you haven't checked my eyes yet," I said.

But he went on with his questions. He wanted to hear about school, about my friends and the games we played, and about the violin. I couldn't figure out why he was so interested in everything. Then he showed me to the waiting room, and asked me if I minded sitting there alone for a while so he could talk to my parents some more. They closed the door behind them, and I sat alone in the waiting room. Time passed. Daylight flooded the room through the open window. The furniture was bright, the curtains were bright. I was worried that I would be afraid, as I was at the conservatory when my mother left me and I was alone. But it was all right in the doctor's waiting room, I was getting used to the bright furniture, and I strained to hear what they were talking about in the other room behind the heavy door. But all I heard was the rumble of the traffic outside. Ages passed, and I wished it would be over so we could go back to normal life. But normal life was spoiled beyond repair, and it wouldn't do to pretend otherwise.

At long last they opened the door and the doctor patted my shoulder and said good-bye. I asked, "When are you going to check my eyes?" and he smiled blandly. I walked outside with my parents. As soon as we were on our way, my mother scolded me for being rude to the doctor and embarrassing her very much. I didn't understand what she meant.

"When the doctor asked if you bite your nails, you said, 'You're crazy.'"

"No I didn't. I said 'THAT'S crazy!'"

"No," said my mother, "You did not. You said "YOU'RE crazy!'"

My protestations were all in vain. My father rested his hand on the back of my neck, and we walked the streets of Haifa in the afternoon light. But even my father's hand wasn't much comfort in the face of such a howling injustice.

My father said, "Why is it so important?"

But my mother was firm. I hated her. I knew that she was wrong and I was right. The injustice of it. Her pain weighed against mine, her failure against mine. Here we were, two people, antagonizing each other, mistrusting each other, thinking only of ourselves. She accused me of forgetting my manners, and worse, of allowing this sinister defect to mar my features unimpeded, and surely weakness of character was what brought it on, and where it would end was anybody's guess. But I knew I was right, and I would never surrender. I held on for dear life and looked to my father in desperation, and he smiled back at me with sympathy and confidence. It was a most important smile. We had formed an alliance against her. Now she had to face us both. She had made up her mind though, and, alas, no one could change it. She was unhappy and I thought it was because of her mistaken idea that I had been rude to the doctor. We walked into a German café downtown and they ordered hot chocolate for me and coffee for themselves.

My mother forgot my bad manners and smiled at me, though her pleasure was not unalloyed. "I'm afraid we'll have to stop your violin lessons for a while," she said. I thought this was punishment for my so-called rudeness, and I raised my eyes in appeal to my father; I knew he wouldn't lead me astray. But he confirmed it.

What bothered me was not so much the discontinuation of my lessons, but the injustice of it, and all because of a mistake, and because we didn't trust each other.

"The doctor said you should stop for a while, because it has a harmful effect on your eyes," my father explained.

"I didn't say 'YOU'RE crazy!' I said 'THAT'S crazy!'"

"It isn't important," said my mother, much to my surprise.

And if this was no longer important, the order of importance of everything was open to question. I gazed at this man and woman I loved most dearly, and I wondered if they were really mine. Twilight permeated the café and a pleasant breeze drifted through. In the street, workers hurried home, carrying their briefcases. An elderly lady at a nearby table buried her face in a German-language paper bound in a wooden frame with reading handles. An atmosphere of suspicion settled into the quiet spaces of the café.

"For how long?" I inquired.

"Until the blinking goes away," replied my father. "Let's hope it won't be long."

"You can stop after the recital," my mother said.

The recital for the end of the year of the Haifa Conservatory was two weeks away.

They were especially nice to me, emphatically nice, but the disappointment they were trying so hard to conceal was contagious, and I felt the futility of it all. Still, it was heartwarming to be bound together by a common destiny. I said no more, I remember; I wasn't going to beg for a reprieve.

My teacher Mrs. Chanina cheered me throughout the final lesson, and wished me luck in the upcoming recital. According to her, it wouldn't do me any harm to have some time off; as a matter of fact, I would probably take up my lessons with redoubled enthusiasm and even more splendid results. I stood before her with downcast eyes, and she caressed my neck. I didn't look at her as we were saying good-bye, and I didn't even turn around for a last look at the house as we were leaving. It just didn't feel like a separation. It was all so meaningless, a trifling matter, a silly technicality. But I never returned to the house, and I was destined to see my teacher Mrs. Chanina only one more time, the night of the recital.

She was in the front row with the other teachers, and we were somewhere in the middle. I remember sitting between my parents, bursting with the anticipation of Uri's performance, as though I was finally about to cancel a debt to myself, a debt of incomprehensible longing. As the outstanding pupil at the conservatory, he was due to appear last, to crown the evening. I watched him sitting there with his family, wearing a white shirt and long blue trousers, his hair combed neatly and parted at the side. He didn't show any signs of being nervous. He was probably twelve or thirteen at the time, but I considered him very grown-up. I remembered how I'd listened from my hiding place to the music flowing out into the dingy corridor, and how I'd come to idolize him. How handsome he looked when he played the violin, how masterful and sure, and everything about him was gracious, sublime, unattainable, ideal. The way he sat, for instance, between his elderly parents, flanked by an older brother and sister in their distinguished row: their earnest faces, the clothes they wore, the way they nodded to the music, and applauded at the end of each piece, how perfectly beautiful it was. Sometimes between performances, one of them would lean over and address a question or comment to Uri, but it was impossible to guess what they were saying.

Toward the end of the recital, Uri stood up, and accompanied by the well-wishing of his family, he left the hall. Mrs. Duniah-Weizman, principal of the Haifa Conservatory, introduced each of the players with a personal anecdote that was sure to please the guests and relations in the audience. Now it was Uri's turn, and the atmosphere grew festive and formal. The accompanist with the curly hair and glasses entered first, followed by Uri, holding his violin. Mrs. Duniah-Weizman raised her head and waited for absolute silence. At last, without further ado, she pronounced Uri's name, the name of the accompanist, and the piece they were going to play, the "La Follia" variations by Corelli.

Uri folded a handkerchief on his chin rest, and his violin sparkled beneath the platform lights. He tucked his instrument under his chin and raised his bow. He closed his eyes, he seemed to concentrate, opened his eyes, and with a nod from his accompanist began to play.

The sadness of the music swelled through the hall and was heightened by the trills at the end of each phrase. Something mysterious transformed the feverish and apparently happy dance into a sort of a desperate yet majestic dirge. Uri's hand was full of controlled emotion and inner strength. Never in my life had I heard such beautiful playing, almost terrifying in its purity, provocative, utterly dispassionate, both cool and ecstatic. And as the rhythm accelerated, the tall boy in the white shirt, blue trousers and grown-up shoes appeared to be wrestling mysterious forces. Sometimes he looked troubled, but it was only the exertion of a flawless performance, sounding the quickening sequence of chords with his nimble fingers. His concentration was so deep that it took him away from the platform and from the many eyes that were watching him, away from the piece itself, from its darkness, wildness, menace. He stood there, the paragon of an ordered world.

I felt how something happened within me, how I was enthralled. I could not immerse myself in the music, not completely, the beauty was unbearable. I watched the attentive audience, I looked at their eyes, I scanned the recital hall, and apprehensively, I peeped at the two closed doors. I knew that any minute now somebody was likely to run in screaming: Stop it! Stop the music! And I knew who that would be. I'd seen him many times on Kings Street, that crazy old beggar, and I couldn't get him out of my mind. I knew he was crouching behind the doors. The audience will be in an uproar, Uri's violin will shake in his hands, the pianist will faint, Uri will raise his head, stop playing, his face pale with guilt and indignity. I saw his parents and his brother and sister as they listened, somewhat numb and unconcerned. But how they will recoil when the wild man rushes through the doors and pounces on the platform screaming: Stop it! Stop it now! Mrs. Duniah-Weizman sat in the front row with the teachers, nodding her head to the rhythm of "La Follia." Little did she know what lurked out there. But I could see him, I saw his fists strike the air, as he waited for the crucial moment. He an old man, dressed in rags, with murderous red eyes and a violent face.

One variation followed another, and I sat there feeling puny and exposed. I felt my father's eyes resting on me briefly, and I searched them for signs of rebuke, in case he had seen the dread on my face, or something queer in my behavior. I listened to the terrible silence all around. The piano and violin hewed away in that terrible silence, and the audience was resting like the dead, in row upon row of family and friends, waiting for a verdict of some sort, waiting with the calmness of despair. I look around. Now my mother takes a handkerchief and wipes a tear from the corner of her eye. She is prone to displays of emotion, especially while listening to music, but this time I believe she's crying over me. I look down at my clothes, at my best short trousers, nicely ironed, at my shining laced-up shoes, and I hate them, I hate them, I hate their intimacy, their affinity, their solemnity, I hate their ridiculous, petty pretentiousness. I raise my eyes to the burnished doors, where someone calculates the perfect entrance. I am sweetly, wildly breathless with anxiety, and I try to turn my attention to the marvelous music and forget all the rest, to capture these moments as they flit by forever. But the circle of brightness is impenetrable, for everything rebounds to the hall, to the danger behind the doors. And the danger does not materialize. Any minute now he'll make his entrance. He's rehearsing his part now, practicing the bitter shout at the audience who are unwitting accomplices to a terrible injustice: Stop the music! Stop it at once! I demand justice! Start the concert again. Start all over again!

But this is not what he intended to say. There's something else, and while he ponders, biding his time behind closed doors, the music nears conclusion, and my heart is pounding with apprehension that he still might break in, and I pray the piece will soon be over before he commits the crime. Yet another variation, and his fist freezes in midair instead of battering the panels of wood. His eyes are red like a killer's eyes, the enormity of his task is paralyzing him, he gasps and groans, and the filthy cloak around his shoulders ripples with the heaving of his chest, and tufts of grizzly hair jut through the slashes in his shirt. I knew the man, I knew him well. How often had I noticed him at his downtown station, drawn to suffer the sight of him as we passed him by, but I never dreamed that someday he would be linked to the recital. Can he create such a terrible infamy? Will he dare? And here it is happening.

There was a deafening noise that threatened to bring the building down. The last strains of the music died and the audience rose and applauded. It was almost cataclysmic. My parents were applauding too, with radiant faces. The pianist with the curly hair and glasses took a bow, and Uri at her side with violin and bow in his left hand stared directly at the audience. The trace of a smile was perceptible on his face, exhausted though he was after so much concentration and detachment, and he squinted at the blinding platform lights like someone who has just woken up and doesn't quite know where he is yet, and a certain gesture of his free right hand seemed to say, "What am I doing here with all these people?"

The doors were opened, and no one was there. The audience applauded on and on. Mrs. Duniah-Weizman helped Uri off the platform, and she hugged him. My mother smiled at me in great satisfaction, and my father took my hand and led me to the door. My mother said Corelli was probably one of the greatest composers. Pupils, teachers, and families clustered throughout the hall, chattering, laughing and shaking hands. By the doors, we ran into Mrs. Chanina. She patted my head affectionately and drew me aside. Her touch was pleasing, and I thought she seemed a little flustered though I couldn't tell why. She leaned down and whispered in my ear, "Music will always be your consolation." Maybe she said that to all her former pupils, or maybe she divined something. Suddenly I knew that here it was, the moment of separation I had avoided the day of our last lesson, in all its pathos. And I knew that I would never again set eyes on this warmhearted, majestic woman, who was so dear to me. I wanted to cry, but I had lost my bearings, so I closed my eyes and made believe that everything would come to a standstill until it was safe to open them again. When I did open my eyes, my teacher Mrs. Chanina was gone, and my parents led me out into the night. We made our way to the bus stop.

It was a warm summer night, and a pleasant sea breeze caressed our faces. We strolled in silence, still thinking about the recital, lost in our private musings. I was glad we weren't talking. The night air was like a soothing balm. I felt it in my limbs, it was almost as if someone else had cried my tears for me and I was purified. I looked at my parents and imagined that the three of us had lately escaped from a dangerous, seductive dream. My hand felt secure in my father's hand. And then I realized that deep inside me I was happy my lessons had been stopped. Did I not know that the happiness was—for the first time in my life—a sigh of relief, of letting go, of accepting? It was a happiness of matters being taken out of my hands, willy-nilly, I was free. But then I experienced it differently: I felt that I was reunited with my parents as we walked to the bus stop, that we were bound together by a new destiny, and our recent trials could no longer stand in our way.

Some months later we left Haifa and moved back to our town. And that Sabbath afternoon in autumn as we set forth from my Great-Aunt Frieda's house, I recalled the aroma of colophony and all the hope and longing it had stirred in me. I asked my parents if I could take up my violin lessons again, and the memory of colophony revived me like a mysterious potion. Even as I write these words I feel an upsurge of hope and expectancy, almost as if I were waiting for the return of someone I loved, who was all but lost and yet nearer and dearer than ever before, or as if I were waiting for some new, redeeming turn of events, however unlikely, with the promise of romance and adventure.

Some time later, the first rains fell. I stood in my room, watching the rain outside my window. I opened my eyes as widely as I could, and stared at the gray light. I tried to count to twenty without blinking. The ordeal seemed to take on a heavy significance, and as I counted nine, ten, I trembled, my eyes brimmed over, and everything was blurry. I was dizzy, the room was spinning round and round to the rhythm of my heartbeat.

Just then, my mother walked into the room and stood behind me.

"What are you doing?"

"Nothing."

"Aren't you doing your homework?"

I didn't turn around to face her. "I'm thinking," I said.

"And just what are you thinking about so hard?" she asked, not unkindly. She approached the window, and looked at my face.

"I was just trying to see if I remember anything about the violin. But I don't. Zero. Nothing. I was trying to remember Schubert's "Musical Moment," that was the last thing I played in Haifa, but I don't remember any of the notes, or what the left hand does, or the fingering, or anything. I'll have to start from the beginning."

She didn't answer. She looked rather doubtful and also baffled. Tears were flowing over my cheeks, and I said, "If I start playing again, the blinking will probably go away. I really think it might."

"It will go away in a few years anyhow," said my mother.

"How do you know?"

"The doctor said so then."

And then I remembered the doctor, and our quarrel over my rudeness, and I felt injured again.

"Then why did my lessons have to stop?"

She made inquiries and found that Mr. Alfredi was the best violin teacher in our town. That evening when my father came home from work, it was decided that my mother would take me to Mr. Alfredi's the following day and sign me up for lessons. The rains continued all night long, but when I came home from school the next day, it wasn't raining anymore and I was very excited. But it started raining again in the afternoon, and my mother, who wanted to postpone our excursion for better weather, understood my sorrows. I put on my poncho and she fastened my hood, tied a kerchief around her head, and took her umbrella. Thus we ventured out into the mud and the pouring rain.

"If anyone knew where we were going in this flood, they'd think we were crazy!" said my mother. But she didn't sound reproachful in the least, she was mischievous, my partner in a silly escapade. Hardly anyone else was abroad in the flood. Mr. Alfredi's house was all the way over on the western border of the town, and our house was in the east. East to west, we trudged against the wind that splattered our faces with rain and our clothes were soaked. We held hands in our joint struggle against the forces of nature and my mother laughed and shouted so that I would hear her behind the curtain of wind and rain and the barrier of my hood, "We're crazy! You know that, we're crazy!"

When we arrived at the first-floor apartment that was Mr. Alfredi's music school, no one was there. We went through the porch that led to his door, and found it locked. There was a note tacked on it: "No lessons today on account of my aunt's funeral. Alfredi." My mother smiled and said, "We're out of luck." She may have been referring to our futile walk through the pouring rain, or she may have felt that the aunt's funeral falling this very day was inauspicious. We waited a while longer on the porch, sheltered from the wind and rain, and I tried to peep through the shutters and see what the room was like inside, but it was too dark. Suddenly we heard peculiar noises coming from the hallway near the porch, sounds of thrashing and thumping and groaning. We hurried to the hallway, and in the semidarkness at the foot of the stairs, we stumbled over violin cases and music books in disarray, and buffeting bodies that wriggled and tangled in a heap. My mother switched the light on, and we watched as three children froze abruptly on the floor like some animal with multiple limbs holding its breath. We saw that they were three boys piled on top of each other, wearing blue ponchos. My mother yanked the uppermost by the arm, and as he scrambled to his feet, the boy who was under him also rose, and they gasped and panted and slapped the dust off their ponchos. The third boy trembled as he continued to lie on the floor, and tucked his head between his knees in fear or pain. My mother tried to help him up, but he obstinately refused assistance, shifted his shoulders, and trembled all the more. My mother bent over him and tried to find his face. She coaxed him until he finally stood up. He was a small, skinny boy, much younger than the other two.

"Who are your parents?" my mother charged the older two, who were grunting vindictively in the corner. "Who are your parents? I want to have a word with them."

The older one, a dark-haired boy with shifty eyes, giggled insolently and didn't answer her. The other, who was fat and rosy-cheeked, said, "That'll show him he's not so hot."

My mother glanced anxiously at the skinny little boy, to see if he was hurt.

"They broke my fingers!" he bawled in a rage of self-pity. "They did! They broke my fingers so I wouldn't be able to play." He cried and fretted primly over his hands. "They were trying to break my fingers!" He held them out for my mother to see, and she examined them with some concern, but there were no signs of injury. "Now I'll never be able to play, and Mr. Alfredi is going to have something to say about that!" he added.

The two older boys stood in the corner looking chastened, and the dark one with the shifty eyes took one cautious step in the direction of the door, while the fat one with the rosy cheeks tugged nervously at his poncho with a sideways glance at the skinny boy to see how he was faring.

The dark one said, "He started it. He always does." My mother looked at the pale skinny boy and said to the older two, "You should be ashamed of yourselves, big strong boys knocking him down like that in the dark."

They gathered their music and violin cases, and we all stepped out on the porch to wait for the end of the storm.

"There's nothing wrong with your fingers, Yoram, and stop bawling," said the dark one. "Let me see."

Yoram held his hands out gingerly and winced with pain. His eyes were pale, too pale, and his hair was blond and cropped. The dark one looked at the fingers and announced, "There's nothing wrong with him, he's a liar!"

"We were just messing around," said the fat one, trying to placate my mother. "We always do and nothing ever happens."

"And does Mr. Alfredi permit this sort of thing?" asked my mother.

The two boys grinned sheepishly and Yoram leaned against the railing hugging his violin case and contemplating the interminable rain. "When Mr. Alfredi finds out," said Yoram deep in contemplation, "he'll kick you out like dogs." They laughed.

After a while the older two, who were tired of waiting for the rain to stop, tied their hoods, hid their violin cases under their ponchos, and walked out to the road. Yoram followed suit and tried to catch up with them, and finally we saw the three disappearing around the bend.

Next day the rain had stopped, and my mother and I set off once more for Mr. Alfredi's music school. As we entered the room, Mr. Alfredi was demonstrating a difficult passage for the dark boy with the shifty eyes. Then the dark boy lifted his bow and repeated the passage. Mr. Alfredi noticed our presence and motioned us to be seated and wait. It seemed that the boy was a new pupil, but he played remarkably well. My mother looked at the teacher. He was very tall, with reddish-gray hair, a long sharp face, and a big nose the tip of which seemed to have worn away. I thought him very ugly and I saw by the look on my mother's face that she was no more favorably impressed with the man. When the boy had finished playing the passage, he looked up and smiled at us disarmingly as though he feared we would tell on him. Mr. Alfredi assigned him an exercise, and the lesson ended abruptly.

I tried to think about my teacher Mrs. Chanina's house in Haifa, but my memories of a few years before were as vague as a distant dream. All I could recall was the color of the braid that rolled down her neck and the furniture that stood out against the background of white walls. And one thing more: the sensual quivering of her nostrils, the faint quivering probably only I could discern, when she narrowed her eyes in ecstasy. I also remembered what she had said at the recital and I wondered if I would understand someday. Mr. Alfredi's studio was small and shabby, and the dilapidated wooden shutters outside creaked in the wind. We were sitting on a most peculiar sofa with an even more peculiar rug covering it, surrounded by an odd assortment of chairs, some of them folding chairs. My mother gave Mr. Alfredi an account of my musical accomplishments, but he didn't seem to be very impressed.

Looking at him more closely, I could see the great freckles that covered his face and the pockmarks on his long, corroded nose. His small, watery eyes had no definite color. He put a training violin in my hands, flipped the pages of a music book, and asked me to play whatever I could remember.

I stared at the music and at the violin in my hands, and I didn't remember anything. Nothing flashed out of the not-so-distant past in my moment of trial. All was lost, my work had gone for nothing. I stood numbly, looking from Mr. Alfredi's countenance which expressed doubt and derision to the little violin I was holding in my hands. Mr. Alfredi asked me to play a note, any note. I drew the bow over one of the strings, and a sound came out that was so hideous I dropped the bow at once and looked at the floor.

"What did you play then?" asked Mr. Alfredi. "What pieces did you play in Haifa, what exercises?" I opened my mouth, but I was speechless. I racked my brains for the name of one of those pieces, but I couldn't remember. After a long silence, Mr. Alfredi turned to my mother and said, "We seem to have forgotten everything." My eyes implored her to come to my assistance. My mother said, "He did play Schubert's 'Musical Moment' at the recital, and Mrs. Duniah-Weizman said . . ."

Mr. Alfredi interrupted, "We'll have to start all over again. He doesn't remember anything." He looked incredulous. A little girl pupil had walked into the studio, and I was overcome with embarrassment as the conversation proceeded.

"And why do you blink like that all the time?" asked Mr. Alfredi. "Is that nice, huh? How do you suppose you'll ever become a violinist and play in a concert when you go blink, blink, blink all the time?"

The girl giggled quietly and hid her face behind her hand. There was a golden heart-shaped ring on that cupped little hand.

"Never mind," said my mother on our way home, "he's an excellent teacher, that's all that counts."

And Mr. Alfredi did in fact prove to be an excellent teacher, and a pleasant man at that. When I got used to him, I even found him charming. How incongruous was that gangly body of his when he stood to play the violin. Suddenly limp and helpless, wheezing and moaning so noisily he all but drowned out the pianissimos, he seemed to be on the point of expiration. And his left wrist wobbled to produce a vibrato, and a frightful pathos sealed his eyes and took his breath away till he seemed about to collapse on the floor. Then just in time, he would breathe his fill, and moan with every sweep of the bow. I didn't particularly care for the cloying emotions Mr. Alfredi displayed at the most inappropriate passages and even the dullest of études. I began to dislike those displays of emotion in music and displays of emotion of any kind. When I first heard Yoram play, I was amazed. So young, and already Mr. Alfredi's best pupil. But I didn't like his playing either. He gave a perfect imitation of his teacher. In fact he surpassed Mr. Alfredi's technique and even outdid his emotionalism. He ran through complicated chords and difficult transitions with astonishing ease, and the charm of a real child prodigy. And when he played the slow, expansive movements, he echoed Mr. Alfredi's histrionic style and even transcended it.

Yoram's whiny vibrato and the tragic accents of his bow were sickening somehow. It was indecent, the way he bared himself with charms so stale and calculated. I began to suspect that inside this pale, skinny little boy lurked an old buffoon who would stoop to any trick in the book to hook his audience. Still, I couldn't help admiring his courage. Dauntless, he defied the world and its conventions. There was something of the trained monkey about him when he played—freakish, gaudy, suspect, but heroic, too, in his audacity.

I myself never learned to play with vibrato. No matter how we tried, Mr. Alfredi and I, my wrist would always turn to stone at the critical moment. He loosened my left elbow, checked my grip, but nothing worked. I knew it wasn't the real thing without a vibrato, though I supposed it might be achieved with a little more reserve. Mr. Alfredi said it would come in time, but one, two, three years went by and no vibrato. Was it perhaps my aversion to displays of emotion that inhibited the movement of my wrist? But why then was I no more successful when I practiced alone at home? Maybe I already knew that I would never be a great violinist, not even Mr. Alfredi's prize pupil. I soon found out that pupils come and pupils go, but I will always be among the second-best. I was convinced that "disability" with the vibrato was the chief stumbling block to my progress, and it was convenient to lay the blame on a mere technical failure. Still, Mr. Alfredi did decide that I would play second violin with Yoram in the Bach double concerto for the recital at the end of the year.

Though Yoram lived on my street, we hadn't met till the day of the flood, the day my mother and I found him in a scrimmage with the other two boys, hollering "They were going to break my fingers so I wouldn't be able to play!" Yoram and I went to different schools, and he was several years younger. He asked if we could have some rehearsals at his house, and I agreed. Yoram and his parents lived in a one-room apartment on the first floor of a two-story house with a yard. A clump of bushes growing wild in the yard and a grove of tall casuarina trees planted by the road obscured the house from view.

Now as I approach the house in my imagination, I stop under the tall old tress and see the house behind the bushes. I am rooted to the spot. The sight distresses me. I can't breathe.

An oppressive week has gone by, and a baffling anxiety prevents me from continuing this story. I feel restless. I can't concentrate. I sit for hours by my typewriter, but my fingers are as sluggish as my mind. I counsel myself, skip this section, go on to the next, but I can't shake off this sense of oppression, and there is no getting around it. I shall have to face the memory and discover what underlies my anxiety, and only then will I be free. The old casuarina trees in front of Yoram's house figure in three incidents in this story: the rehearsal at Yoram's house, the Eitan episode, and the great scene which always reminds me of a folk play. But which of these three incidents transmits these waves of anxiety? Again and again, I come up against a brick wall, and I have trouble breathing.

I can remember many similar attacks of anxiety, and on each occasion, I knew the cause lay in something I had ignored, either in thought or deed. I also knew that I must struggle to penetrate the moment that gave rise to the feeling, to untie the knot, to restore the moment to its true proportions which are usually not so large as they appear later. I was not always successful, but when I was, the wheel turned back, I faced the moment and settled my accounts with it, and as a result, I experienced a marvelous sense of well-being, as if a lost possession had found its way back to me or as if a bitter, long-standing quarrel had finally been settled. But this moment, where shall I find it, where did it go, and what has it to do with the story I'm trying to tell? It taps me on the shoulder, and demands satisfaction, and holds me under the shade of old casuarina trees in front of Yoram's house.

It's late, my house is locked, and I put a record on to drown out the noise of the air conditioner. It's very hot outside. At times, the stubborn hum of the air conditioner can be like a dreary lullaby to the silence. But at this painful moment it sounds more like a ferocious beast, mocking my unhappiness. Funny how this phantom pain will emanate from inanimate objects that have not yet been contaminated. And now, the page in my typewriter is rising line by line.

A week has gone by, and I feel better. I try to visualize the path that leads to the bushes, the overgrown bushes that hide the first floor of the house from the road. The tiles on the floor were cracked and broken. I knocked on the door. Yoram's mother answered. She was pale and skinny like her son, and her movements were unnecessarily brusque. Yoram wasn't home, much to my surprise, although we'd made a date to rehearse. His mother said he would be home soon and asked me to sit down and wait for him, despite his bad manners. She showed me where to put my violin, and interrogated me about my family, and I suppose she was satisfied, because she left me alone in the room. I don't remember what the room looked like, but I do remember that it was dark there in the early afternoon, perhaps because the bushes in front of the house kept out the light.

Yoram's mother walked in again a little while later and I saw that she was much older than my mother. Her hair was gray, her face was wrinkled, and her back was bowed. She looked nothing like Yoram. She sat down beside me, and faced me.

"What do you think?" she began abruptly. "He won't get him home in time, and he knows he has a rehearsal, if you don't mind."

I began to feel uncomfortable.

"What a sense of timing. You think all that equipment he buys him will do any good? Now, just before the recital? It won't do any good at all, if you don't mind. What does he want from him? Tell me? Let him practice in peace. But not him, no, not him, he buys him all those rifles and pistols and all those complicated boxes, the main thing is he shouldn't have his mind on the violin. Is that how they raised Yehudi Menuhin? Is that how they raised Yasha Heifetz? Never! And he wants him to go out for sports at the Junior Maccabbee Club, if you don't mind. Who needs it? You think it does his hands any good? A violinist has to have the most sensitive hands in the world, if you don't mind. But he's afraid he'll grow up like a girl. Who ever heard such nonsense, grow up like a girl. Playing the violin makes you a girl? Are Yehudi Menuhin and Yasha Heifetz girls?" She hooted in triumph.

She didn't wait for my reply, but said, "If you want you can wait for Yoram outside," as if she'd noticed something about me. "You have to practice for hours and hours. You have to be dedicated. Otherwise it's no good. If you're not dedicated, you're wasting your time, right? Because later the hands get hard and rough and crooked, and then it's too late. Even Mr. Alfredi doesn't understand. God!" She clasped her hands. "God in heaven! Nobody understands. They see but they keep quiet. They don't care. They see it under their very noses, but they turn away. You have to throw it in their faces. You have to pry their hearts open, you have to break in like a thief to make them understand, right? You can go outside and wait," she said, and opened the door for me.

I sat on the front stairs and finally Yoram and his father showed up, empty-handed. I stood to greet them. Yoram's father was short and skinny, and he wore a visor cap. When he looked at me I saw his eyes were cold and pale like his son's, and also very proud. We went into the house and Yoram's father left us in the room. Yoram was quiet. He took out his violin and rubbed his bow with colophony, and mumbled something to himself. We tuned our violins and began to play Bach's double concerto. A few minutes later Yoram's father stood in the doorway yelling, "Horrible! Disgusting!" He stared at me in revulsion, in accusation, and slammed the door shut. Yoram stood still for a moment concentrating, and then asked me to start again from the beginning, because, he said, my entrance was a little off. We began it again. We had practiced so often with Mr. Alfredi that we rarely needed to interrupt our playing with corrections. In the slow, pensive second movement, where the second violin answers the first, as if echoing it, Yoram was playing with his usual emotional vibrato when suddenly we heard a prolonged scream behind the door. Yoram stopped playing and hurried to the door carrying his violin to see what his mother's screaming was about. I stood alone in the room and I was frightened. I heard doors opening and closing and the sound of muffled voices, and another piercing scream that rang in my ears like the cry of a wounded animal. Yoram's father stalked in, looking as unruffled and proud as he had before. He said, "You'd better go home now, Yoram is busy. Come back another time."

He waited while I packed my violin, and walked me to the door. In the hallway I heard her scream again, and this time I heard what she was screaming—"Murderer! Murderer!" And then the door closed behind me.

When I got home I was too ashamed to tell my parents what I'd seen and heard at Yoram's house. I was old enough to keep my secrets. But I remember that I watched them out of the corner of my eye. They were busy at whatever they were doing, and I answered them in silence, made them swear on oath to always let me have my way. But they weren't paying any attention to me. How easy it was to watch them like this, to watch their every move. But as I did so I became aware that my power over them was strictly limited. I dreaded the unknown, the equivocal, unforeseeable times to come. I went to my bedroom and stared out the window. The light was fading. For some reason, my father's old grandmother who had died long ago suddenly entered my mind. I remembered the way she used to sit in her armchair, far away from everything and everyone around her. My father's uncle, her own son, claimed that all she ever thought about was the Messiah, and maybe he was guessing, or maybe she had revealed something to him. But she had always looked to me like a phantom sitting there, an optical illusion. She was no longer a part of her surroundings. She had felt the touch of grace and was preparing for the fabulous journey that lay ahead. As I stood in my room watching twilight fall, I recognized for the first time in my life that the painting hanging over my great-grandmother's armchair, the painting of a pampered bird languishing in its own blood, was a painting of Death. Now I understood why I had always associated it with the old woman in the chair. It was a secret treaty, a covenant of redemption. Till now, death had only meant the disaster that would take away the man and woman I loved so much, as it had taken my grandfather away from me. Sometimes I would wake up in the middle of the night terrified by a vision that disappeared almost immediately and strain to hear them breathing in their room, afraid they might be taken from me in their sleep. But this evening after the rehearsal with Yoram I was stunned by a new discovery—I knew no more about them than they knew about me. I could watch them and threaten them silently as much as I cared to but I could never turn back the clock to the days when their lives were centered around me. They had their secrets, and their secrets would follow them from now on like shadows, beyond my control. This made me feel a little helpless and nostalgic, but also excited, for anything could happen now that I was on my own, and everything was waiting for me, I only had to mature and be all on my own. I sat there thinking in the darkness of my room when all of a sudden my mother opened the door.

"What are you up to, sitting there in the dark doing nothing?"

I turned around anxiously to face her, as if she'd caught me out, and I didn't know what to answer. She switched on the light looking puzzled and angry, and I was furious with her for calling me to account like that. I tried to look upon her as some vaguely familiar stranger.

"I feel like it," I said.

"Who ever heard of such a thing, sitting in the dark, staring out the window, doing nothing?" said my mother. "That's absolutely unheard of. Idleness is the mother of evil. Idleness leads to decadence."

"I want a little decadence," I said.

After my initial anger had worn off, I decided that I should adopt the art-of-living-together policy, to pay less attention to her. I felt an urgent need to do something, I knew not what. She stood in my room for a while, looking amazed. Was she perhaps confused to learn that the old rules no longer applied? Was she disconcerted?

"You don't practice nearly enough," said my mother. "A week from now you're playing with Yoram in the recital. You have a responsibility, have you not? Do you want him to show you up in front of everyone?"

"It'll be okay, don't worry."

"Well, someone has to worry. And it will not be okay, because you couldn't care less."

Was my declining interest in the violin already so apparent? She had interrupted my thoughts when she entered the room, and those thoughts seemed infinitely precious to me now. This new impetus to attend to my own thought processes, to question my status vis-à-vis the others, held the promise of a vast field of discovery, for me alone, and I was eager to get on with it. I had to do something now, immediately, and I needed absolute privacy. But what did I want to do? And then something incredible happened, something that led me to believe in the invisible mover, the hand that guides my footsteps in a meaningful progression.

Next door was my uncle's house with its big Hebrew library. I had often browsed through his books and had even borrowed some of them. Having nothing better to do just then, I wandered over to my uncle's house and looked through the books in his library. I picked a book off the shelf and opened it at random. The author was G. Shofman, and I had never noticed the book before. My eyes fell on the heading: *The Violin.*

"I do not care for this instrument and I hereby challenge its sovereignty. It is enough to consider the way it is played, by rubbing two surfaces against each other, to send shivers of revulsion up the spine. Certain low notes and transitional tones are especially unpleasant to the ear. The strings, incidentally, are made from animal tissue! This is also somewhat repulsive.

"I suppose one ought to consider the excellence of such famous instruments as the Stradivarius played by virtuosi (though I suggest we might be critical even here!), but as for the cheap variety in the hands of pupils—a harmonica would be preferable! In the latter case of violin we have to bear with a mournful scream, a sniveling plea for mercy that is enough to induce a severe case of melancholia.

"Yes, melancholia. The nightmare of the Jewish Ghetto screams out of these fiddles. The Diaspora Jew practically venerated the violin, it was his sine qua non, *Yidel mit'n fidel.* In every Jewish household, the beloved son, whether he was gifted musically or a complete imbecile, had to 'saw away' on his violin, for the pleasure of his mother, who found her greatest fulfillment in the violin. Come what may, the violin prevailed. Trials and tribulations, every kind of care and woe, debts, installments, bill collectors—and the violin!"

I read these words by Shofman, and my heart began to pound. Was it just a coincidence? I thought about the disgraceful rubbing of surfaces against each other, and the Diaspora Jew in his ghetto, sniveling and begging for mercy, and I smoldered. I read the paragraph over and over and over again. At last I made up my mind what to do. I had found myself a worthy enterprise: to stop my violin lessons.

For the time being I kept this decision to myself. I didn't want to inform my parents. Not yet. I was afraid it would make them very sad. What sacrifices they had made for my violin lessons in those times of austerity, and what happiness my progress had given them. But it had to be done. I didn't know when yet. First I had to get through the recital.

A few days before the recital we rehearsed at Mr. Alfredi's together with our accompanist. My heart wasn't in it. Since reading Shofman's article I could barely suppress my loathing for the instrument. But to my great amazement, I found that I was playing more fluently and accurately than I ever had before, as if the music was playing itself without any guidance from me. It was better than ever. I wondered whether anyone else noticed, and after I finished playing the slow, pensive, second movement, Mr. Alfredi clapped his hands and called out to me, "Bravo! Bravo!" He praised me warmly and said that I had evidently been practicing a lot at home. When we went on to the third movement, I was surprised to note what great pleasure the compliment gave me, I had so naively believed that I was indifferent.

After the rehearsal, Mr. Alfredi said he hoped I would play as well at the recital. And I knew the recital would be the grand finale of my musical career.

On our way out of Mr. Alfredi's studio, Eitan, the dark-haired boy with the shifty eyes, followed me. He had waited to hear us play the double concerto after his own rehearsal had ended. Eitan was younger than I, but taller, and he looked as if he knew the secrets of life. We seldom met at Mr. Alfredi's, and when we did, we hardly ever exchanged words. I suspected that he felt unfriendly, if not hostile, toward me, and I usually avoided him.

But as I left Mr. Alfredi's studio, Eitan caught up with me. We walked along in silence. Then Eitan said, "I can't stand the way Yoram plays. He thinks he's the greatest violinist in the world. In my opinion, you played the Bach double better than he did."

I thought he was trying to flatter me, and I couldn't decide what he was driving at.

"Oh, he's got technique," said Eitan, "I'll give him that much. But he plays like a fake. And Mr. Alfredi thinks he's the world's greatest. But what does Mr. Alfredi know? He didn't even get into the Philharmonic orchestra."

I found myself wanting to tell Eitan about my decision to stop taking lessons, but I was afraid. If Mr. Alfredi found out about it, it might not be very pleasant; I didn't want him to know until the last possible moment. I didn't want to estrange him yet.

"Ugh," I said, "the violin. You call that an instrument? Surfaces rubbing against each other, and a horrible, sniveling sound coming out."

Eitan gaped as if he hadn't understood me properly, as if he ascribed some obscure meaning to what I'd said, but he seemed to accept my statement as confirmation of his.

We had walked almost as far as my house when Eitan stopped and said, "I walked you to your house, now you walk me to my house." Eitan lived in the neighborhood by the railway, on the other side of the town. I didn't understand what he wanted. I thought he was joking. I looked at him. He was perfectly serious, and the shifty twinkle was gone from his eyes.

"But I have to go home now. They're waiting for me, they'll worry," I lied.

"Come on," said Eitan, "it'll only take fifteen minutes, come on, it'll be all right."

"I can't," I said.

We stood there doggedly, holding our violin cases, and neither of us would budge. It wasn't late, and I didn't really mind walking him home, but a strong perversity took hold of me, maybe because he sounded so eager and peremptory, and because I had always been suspicious of him. Eitan peered around. He bent over suddenly and dropped his violin case in the middle of the road. Then he looked directly at me with an inscrutable expression. It took me years to figure out what that expression meant. He took a few steps back and said, "I don't care. I'm leaving it here, and if anything happens, it's your responsibility, because you're supposed to walk me home, and you won't, so just remember, if anything happens to my violin, it's your responsibility!"

This was totally unexpected. He actually left his violin case in the middle of the road, turned his back, and walked away. I didn't know what to do. It was my responsibility, he said so. If I didn't move it over to the curb where it wouldn't get run over, terrible things might happen. This was so disturbing that I crouched to pick it up, but Eitan veered around with amazing alacrity and rushed to move his violin back to the middle of the road.

"Don't you dare touch it, you hear? It isn't yours, you have no right to touch it. It isn't yours! If anything happens, it's your responsibility, because you don't keep your promises!"

"I never promised you anything," I objected.

His face was twisting in anger or pain. I was afraid he would hit me. But all he said was, "Come on, walk me home, what do you care? Please. I'll tell you all kinds of things."

With brilliant insight I realized my only chance to escape this predicament was to run for it, and leave him standing in the middle of the road with his violin, and then it would be his responsibility. And as I ran home, I could hear him shout, "Remember, it'll be here all night, and if anything happens it'll be your responsibility, damn you!"

I got home winded and I hoped he wasn't following me to prolong this inane argument. A few minutes later, however, I began to worry that he really had left his violin in the middle of the road. His behavior had certainly been odd. Nobody else behaved like that. I sneaked out to look for him. It wasn't dark yet, but I couldn't see him or his violin. I thought maybe he was lying in ambush in somebody's yard, and I edged along our fence, waiting for him to spring at me. But time passed and nothing happened. I took courage and advanced out into the open, but there was no sign of him. I stopped in front of Yoram's house, under the casuarina trees, and I squinted at the horizon. People were walking to and fro, but Eitan wasn't among them. I figured that as soon as I had left, he'd picked up his violin and gone home. But I wasn't relieved, no, I was old enough to understand what I had done and I was shocked. I was miserable and penitent, and I didn't know what to do. Why was I so bad? I turned my face away from the road so no one would see if I started crying. I was afraid, something had to be done, urgently, but what? I had never given Eitan a second thought, I had only seen him a few times in my life, and yet now he loomed so fatefully over me that I was paralyzed. "Remember, it's your responsibility!" his voice rang in my ears. I had never felt so responsible before. With my back to the road, I could see the bushes in front of Yoram's house.

I considered various excuses to justify myself and prove his irrationality—lame excuses that paled and faltered beside my shame and misery. Whatever I might say in self-defense was countered by the inscrutable expression he wore as he put his violin in the middle of the road. It haunted me for years. In my selfishness I hadn't realized that he was asking for friendship. If only I had been more sensitive he wouldn't have gone to such extremes. I hated myself then as I always hate myself when I realize, too late, too late, that someone is asking for help and friendship. Maybe I lack the faculty to hear the whispers of another's heart, to understand the murmured implications.

During those painful, shameful moments, while I leaned against the trunk of one of the tall old trees, not knowing where to turn or what to do, I could only wonder how in the world I was going to make amends. I wanted nothing better than to stand before him with downcast eyes and say I was sorry, so sorry for the wrong I'd done. And the more I begged him, the more I groveled, the more I would suffer and the less ashamed I would be. But at the time it would have been impossible for me to display emotions of this sort. They were too private, they couldn't be shared. He had to forgive me, it was the only way. Even if he forgot the whole incident, I would be miserable until he pardoned me. I had to see him. I had to see him now. I had to see what he was doing.

This growing need to see him was my only hope to escape from under the trees where I'd been standing heaven knows how long in a state of unprecedented anguish. I finally tore myself away and set off for Eitan's neighborhood.

I thought I would reconnoiter the neighborhood till I spotted him in the window or maybe outside in the yard. I would see what he was up to, but he wouldn't see me. It was getting dark as I carried

my burden of guilt up to the road, and I remember the fresh smell of
dust on that miserable summer evening. When I reached the neighborhood by the railway, I was frightened. It was an unpaved road,
on either side of which were cottages in a row and black wooden
sheds and giant eucalyptus trees. I hoped I might hear a violin somewhere. Maybe he was drowning his sorrows in music, and that way
I would be able to locate his house. Looking up at the glimmering
windows, I walked through the neighborhood, but I couldn't find
him. Hadn't he gone home? Where was he? My guilt was overpow-
ering me and I wandered up and down. Finally I gave up, feeling
very sorry for myself.

I walked home slowly. The more I pitied myself, the less I suffered the agonies of remorse. I pictured myself as a tortured penitent in order to escape the all-pervading memory of Eitan. It was a
contest, and the advantage shifted back and forth. I knew that I
would never be one of those children of "The Heart," those marvelous children I had cried over in bygone days.

I was apprehensive about meeting Eitan at the recital. In a small
room that usually served as the office of the Histadrut Cultural
Building, we unpacked our cases. Mr. Alfredi was nervously giving
out last-minute instructions. A few pale pupils tuned their instruments and rosined their bows. Leaning against a desk in the corner
was Eitan, looking much the same as he always did. The shifty
sparkle in his eyes was back. I wasn't sure I ought to speak to him.
Would he look my way? What would he say to me? It was surprising to see that he hadn't changed in any way. I didn't know
whether to laugh or cry. And perhaps he was only testing me. Maybe
this was just another one of his old tricks. Maybe he'd forgotten
everything. Or was he seething inside and merely saving face? I
stood in the doorway and he smiled his usual noncommittal smile.
I didn't have the nerve to approach him. I put my violin down and
hurried out to sit with my parents in the auditorium.

"You aren't even nervous," said my mother. "That isn't a good
sign. You don't care. You don't care about anything."

Yoram's mother walked into the auditorium and my mother followed her with her eyes. When the gray-haired lady had seated

herself, my mother whispered something I couldn't hear to my father. I knew it was about Yoram's mother. My father nodded a reply and stared at the woman's back. What did they know that I didn't know? But I could only scratch the surface of things. The rest remained unfathomable.

After the recital, as we were leaving the auditorium on our way home, I cautiously mentioned to my parents that maybe I ought to drop my violin lessons, temporarily, of course, so that I could devote more time to my studies at the high school. I thought I noticed my father smiling to himself in the dark as if he'd foreseen this. My mother pretended to be shocked but I could tell their disapproval was not serious.

"I've noticed lately," said my mother, "that you're losing interest in everything. Nothing interests you anymore."

I protested and mentioned my studies again.

My father said, "Do what you think is best."

I told them about G. Shofman's article which I had found in my uncle's library. My mother was horrified at what I had discovered in her beloved brother's library. "Nonsense!" she said. "I don't believe anyone would print such utter nonsense." And of course she was right, but at the time the article had seemed to me the height of reason. My father said, "It doesn't matter. If you want to stop, there's no point in arguing about it."

I had a vague perception of leaving them again, of coming into my own. I wasn't worried anymore about hurting them or breaking faith.

"Remember how I ran with you in the pouring rain like a madwoman?" said my mother. "You were so determined. I thought we'd wait a day or two, but not you, you couldn't wait."

I remembered that rainy day, and it seemed irrelevant just then. I loved my father's calm, his moderation, his sense of proportion, and especially his irony when he said, "You'll go to Mr. Alfredi yourself and tell him about your decision."

"Of course," I said reluctantly. "Yes."

I hadn't thought about that. Once again I understood the growing significance of the word *responsibility*. "Yes," I added as an afterthought, "I'll tell him myself after vacation."

At home I put my violin where I always kept it, and I knew that I would never touch it again.

Mr. Alfredi's summer vacation, which lasted a month or two, began after the yearly recital. One day my mother looked at my face and asked me a question that seemed to come from somewhere far away. "Have you noticed anything about your face?"

I hadn't. But I learned from her expression that my blinking was going away. I found indications of this gradual change in my milieu, but it had nothing to do with what was going on inside me. It was just something external, a meaningless mechanism. When the vacation was over I decided to go to Mr. Alfredi and take my leave of him properly. Once again I set off on the long walk, by the same route with never a detour or shortcut. I felt timid, worried that it would be unpleasant. How could I look in Mr. Alfredi's eyes when I told him the news? He might feel hurt, he might feel deceived after all these years, he might even yell at me. But I knew this was the test of my responsibility, and I would have to face the consequences of living my life as I saw fit. Just as I walked up the path to Mr. Alfredi's music school, another of those mysterious coincidences took place which highlight the symbolism and symmetry of my life.

I heard the old familiar melody. It issued out of eternity, this music I had loved so dearly once, returning to me like an errant lover, strange and discovered anew. I was transfixed. It took me several minutes to identify the piece by name, the "La Follia" variations by Corelli. I hadn't heard it in all the years since the recital at the Haifa Conservatory.

I stood and listened to the muffled sounds emerging from the house. My heart was pounding. I had reached the crossroads. How well I remembered the boy in Haifa who had played the "La Follia" variations, but how difficult it was to recall the boy in the audience who listened to him with so much envy and longing. The music was swelling as I climbed the stairs. Mr. Alfredi was playing all by himself in the studio. He nodded for me to wait. Did he notice I had come without my violin? I listened to him, moaning and wheezing as he always did, and I tried to remember the enigma of the music which had so enthralled me once. But "La Follia" was now a tattered beggar, throwing herself at my mercy, asking me to remember the pride of her youth. But I had other things to think about. Where was the enigma? The more I listened the more I hardened myself against the insipidity of the music and the excessive ardor Mr. Alfredi lent it as he played. Here was another sign that I had made the right decision. The crossroads were behind me, the worst was over.

Mr. Alfredi said, "What a pity. And soon we'll be starting chamber music, and I thought you might switch to the viola." He smiled sweetly. I saw he wasn't angry at all. He wasn't shocked. Maybe I hadn't deceived him. Maybe he was used to it. Maybe that was just the way of things. I told him how difficult school was, that I wanted to devote more time to my studies. Only for a couple of years, of course. And he smiled, and nodded.

We parted amicably, and as I was leaving the house I heard him playing "La Follia" again, though it was hard to imagine why. He didn't even get into the Philharmonic orchestra!

I made my way home, filled with vague new hopes. I was free and happy, optimistic. It was autumn, the time of fresh beginnings, the time I love the best. The High Holidays were drawing near, and with them a poignant expectancy, a flurry in the air. On our street I saw a crowd of people standing under the casuarina trees in front of Yoram's house. As I approached the crowd, I saw Yoram's mother weeping bitterly and someone supporting her arms so she wouldn't collapse. Nearby stood Yoram's father, the invariable visor cap shading his pale, proud eyes. In the center stood Yoram, glancing fitfully from one to the other. Neighbors and passersby were shaking their heads sadly or whispering together. Some of them had taken it upon themselves to brief the newcomers. The scene must have been in progress for some time.

Yoram's mother was clasping her hands and screaming, "Murderer! Murderer! He wants to take my boy away so he won't be a violinist. He wants to ruin him! He wants to turn him into what he is. Save him! Save him from that murderer!"

Yoram's father didn't react. He didn't seem inclined to fight with her. Finally he lost his patience and played his last card. "Yoram," he called, "come with me and you'll get the badge of the Palmach."

I stood on the sidelines hoping Yoram wouldn't notice me. Between the heads of the crowd I saw him look at his father, imploring him not to set such awful temptation in his way. But his father repeated, "Remember, Yoram, the badge of the Palmach!"

Yoram's mother had nothing comparable to offer, and she appealed to the crowd, with only justice and mercy left to rival the badge of the Palmach. "He wants you to think I'm crazy so they'll take my boy away. But I'm not crazy! I'm normal! I won't give that murderer my child! He won't turn him into another murderer!"

The crowd followed these proceedings, inclining first one way, then the other. Some took sides and pleaded for the claimants, others vacillated because it was so difficult to judge.

For a moment I believed Yoram was looking at me. I fidgeted. It was degrading. How could they take their problems out in public, out in the street, I wondered. This scene, skinny little Yoram standing between his parents, pale and torn with indecision, surrounded by the pitying crowd, this scene was unforgettable. A few months before, we had played the Bach double together at the recital, and now he was a stranger. I didn't recognize him, I didn't pity him, and I didn't feel his pain. I was simply disgusted by this shameful display in the street. I refused to have anything to do with it.

"He has the hands of a great violinist!" Yoram's mother screamed. She grabbed his hand and raised it sky-high to prove her point. And Yoram's father said, "If you come with me you'll be a man. If you stay with her you'll go crazy like her."

Yoram lost his head. I saw him wrench away from his mother and stop his ears with both hands. It was a hard choice, between a murderer and a crazy woman. His strength was failing. I couldn't bear to watch any more. I walked away and then turned around for a last look. This time the scene appeared in a new light: it was a theatrical performance. The actors were stuck in their roles, loving every minute of the old drama, the theme of the father and the mother and the child prodigy. I never forgot this scene. Little by little I lost my youthful, haughty contempt and I learned to love the play and the three players who wandered far and wide searching for a sympathetic audience to fight their battles and see justice done. But many years went by before I could understand how much love and compassion were revealed in this play.

When I got home that autumn afternoon I was still disgusted with what I had beheld. My erstwhile hopes had fled.

"I've been noticing lately that your eyes are getting better," said my father, "Sometimes you don't blink at all. Have you noticed?"

I hadn't. I went to look at myself in the little bathroom mirror. What was there to see? I had never been able to see myself blinking. How could I tell that I'd stopped? My face was sealed as usual.

One fine day I stopped scowling and the mysterious malady disappeared. I never understood what brought it on, and I could no more understand why it vanished.

My mother said, "That's what the doctor said. He said it would go away in adolescence."

The word *adolescence* coming from her sounded insulting for some reason.

Then the stigma was gone, and quietude descended on my face forevermore.

Between Night and Dawn

❋

translated from the hebrew by dalya bilu

For Nilly Mirsky
Paris, November 1978

We stood at the open gate and didn't dare to go in. The big yard looked as neglected as ever and likewise the big two-story house standing in the clearing of a sparse old orange grove. The stylish red tile roof recalled the glories of former days, as did the avenue of tall palms leading from the gate to the big steps at the front of the house. Once upon a time "millionaires" lived here. They came from Europe and built themselves a farmhouse on the outskirts of the town in the heart of an orange grove which they intended to improve and cultivate. But before the house was completed, the World War broke out and spoiled their plans. They left and emigrated to America. In the big house remained the poor relations, Pesach's family who had been alloted a corner in one of the wings. They were supposed to look after the estate and take care of the orange grove, but the task was too much for them. The scale and grandeur of the house and the size of the orange grove were immense, and they shut themselves up and huddled in their corner as if they were afraid of being crushed by an avalanche. Pesach's father became a cart driver, while the house, the farmyard and the big orange grove sank with the years into neglect and ruin. We passed the gates quite often. Our eyes grew accustomed to taking in at one glance the house and garden, the ruined fish-pond and avenue of palms, a monument to the legendary millionaires who had passed this way many years before. We knew that somewhere in a corner of the disintegrating house Pesach's family was hiding. Sometimes we saw the horse grazing between the old orange trees or Pesach's mother hanging out washing in the yard. But we never went in.

It was the afternoon of one of the *hamsin* days at the beginning of spring. A strong smell of dust and manure hung in the air. We knew this smell well. It was Pesach's smell. We all agreed that Pesach didn't wash and that he preferred sleeping next to his father's horse. This had been the subject of many jokes in years gone by. But recently the jokes had stopped, either because we had told them so often that we were sick of them, or because we were old enough by now to understand their poor taste, or perhaps Pesach's personality had simply ceased to interest us. When he arrived among us he was older than we were, because he had failed a number of grades, and we had turned him into one of the amusements of our childhood. Our teachers too did not spare him their wit and sarcasm, until they despaired of him and left him to sit among us, a dumb and unaccusing witness to the changes taking place in us, filling our lives with new content and new figures. But as we stood outside the open gate with the smell of dust and manure, familiar but several times more potent, assailing our senses, the memory of the old jokes about Pesach returned.

"There's nothing for it, we have to go in," said Naomi, her round face blushing in an embarrassed smile. But she didn't take a step forward. Instead she looked at Eli Shapira. This was the first time for all of us, and we didn't know what to expect or how to behave; we only knew that we mustn't greet them on our arrival or departure, and on no account could we laugh or even smile. Eli Shapira's blue eyes narrowed slightly as they scanned the avenue of palms before us, like an officer leading his troops into dangerous territory and assessing the length of the road, the dangers, and the chances of crossing it safely.

Arik said: "I don't understand why the whole committee has to go. In my opinion, the four of you represent the five members of the committee very well. I'm sure you'll manage without me. Anyway, I know I'll start laughing. I'm telling you, I always start laughing in situations like that. I know myself, believe me. And I hate all this hypocrisy too. None of you feels any sorrow for Pesach or what happened to him and I can't stand these phoney rituals. Good-bye!"

Eli Shapiro stared at him: "You're coming in with everyone else."

"And try to control yourself and not to laugh," added Naomi, "and don't try to make us laugh either."

"I'm not responsible for what happens to me in there," warned Arik.

"Then it's time you started being responsible," said Rachel Hyman and tossed her head with a haughty expression. She was a very pretty girl, and she knew it, and she was Eli's girlfriend.

Arik felt that he was the object of hostility again. He was sure that the reason for this resentment was that he always dared to express out loud what we all thought in our heart of hearts but didn't have the guts to admit. He was familiar with these frequent shifts between responsiveness and impatience on the part of his audience and he was very attentive to them. However, his buffoonish eagerness for constant applause sometimes got in the way of his efforts to adapt himself quickly to new situations and profit from them.

We entered the palm avenue which had once been paved with big tiles, of which only a few were left, most of them broken. Next to the entrance steps we stopped and looked around. There was no one to be seen at the entrance to the house and we didn't know how to find Pesach's quarters.

"Maybe we should just follow the smell?" suggested Arik in a conspiratorial whisper, returning to the old jokes, and was rewarded by a suppressed smile on the face of Rachel Hyman, but at the sight of Eli's stern expression she immediately frowned and looked disgusted and reproachful. Hypocrites, said Arik to himself, and you're the queen of the hypocrites. He thought that she had a bad influence on Eli. Ever since she had arrived among us she had immediately monopolized Eli and in Arik's opinion spoiled the close friendship between them, which would never be the same again. Arik hated her but he tried not to show it.

"There it is," said Eli and pointed at a side entrance to the left of the house. Not far off stood the cart, with its shafts drooping to the ground.

Eli knocked on the door. It was opened by Pesach's big brother, whom we now saw for the first time. He had disappeared from town years before and there were strange and contradictory stories about him. Some people said that he had been caught stealing and was serving a prison sentence. Others claimed that he hadn't been caught but had succeeded in giving the police the slip at the last minute and had escaped the country disguised as a woman. Still others said that he had taken part in a daring underground action against the British, had been banished to Africa, and set out from there to travel the world. It's also possible, of course, that he had simply moved to another part of the country, and his absence from town had led to the manufacture of all these strange rumors. He too was redheaded like his brother but not clumsy and ugly like Pesach. Naomi said afterwards that she felt something "cold, arrogant and cruel" in the young man's slitty green eyes. He let us in without saying anything. In the room Pesach and his father were sitting alone except for two old women who were both crying bitterly. Pesach stood up when we came in and his father ordered him: "Get more chairs." Pesach went out to fetch the chairs.

One of the old women stopped crying for an embarrassing moment and asked: "Are you from the school?"

"Yes," said Eli.

"None of the teachers have come yet," said Pesach's father, but there was no complaint or bitterness in his voice, it was simply a statement of fact which also held out an assurance that the fault would soon be corrected.

Pesach came back with the chairs. We sat down in a row next to the wall and opposite us sat Pesach and his father and his brother and the two weeping women. For a spell that went on forever we sat in a silence broken only by the groans of the old women and the creaking of Pesach's chair as he shifted restlessly on his seat.

Eli sat with a calm, serious expression on his face and by his side sat Rachel, looking alternately at us and at the mourners sitting opposite us. Naomi looked at the crying old women, she didn't take her eyes off them, and for a moment it seemed to me that she would soon get up and join them and weep with them, her face was so full of sorrow and pain. I shrank on my chair and stared at some invisible point in the room, waiting anxiously for somebody to open his mouth and say something. And perhaps, I thought, it was the custom not to talk in a house of mourning, but in that case too it would be hard to stand this silence for much longer. Out of the corner of my eye I saw Arik watching us, examining our expressions and reactions. He was more interested in us than in Pesach and his mother's death and his grieving family. We were always being subjected to his observations and criticisms. He lay in wait for us, pouncing on every blunder or mistake or slip of the tongue that might come in useful for his jokes or imitations or the skits he wrote for class parties. Now he was apparently collecting material for the barbs he would direct at us when we left Pesach's house.

Pesach broke the silence: "They're the class committee," he said to his father and pointed at us with his finger. "The whole class chose them in a vote."

"Why didn't they choose you?" asked his brother and we didn't know if he was teasing him or asking in all innnocence.

Pesach tittered in embarrassment. He looked like a cat which had been dipped in water, there was something blurred and raw about his appearance. He sat with his hulking body bowed over his knees. His ginger hair was cut without any logic, and big, dark freckles covered his face like a mask. His eyebrows were so fair that they were hardly visible under his narrow forehead, and his eyes were two colorless slits. And nevertheless, at that moment I felt something new in him: the death which had passed through his house had left some mysterious mark on him, shed the light of some other presence on him.

"Is it according to grades?" inquired Pesach's father.

"No!" cried Pesach, "I told you: it's by voting."

"Ha!" his father exclaimed in surprise, but his face did not reveal whether this had solved the problem for him or not.

Arik's eyes glinted gleefully behind the lenses of his glasses. It was hard to tell what was going on in Arik's heart. Perhaps we weren't really interested then in the motivations of our fellows, we were too enthralled by ourselves and what was happening inside us. But these questions bothered me. What was the strange demon darting around inside him, what was the meaning of his eagerness to pounce with such glee on anyone caught in a moment of weakness or failure, why did he always look for the ridiculous in everyone and everything? Was he afraid of his own weakness, of its exposure? What was his weakness? He had built a wall around himself and his life with us was like a constant flight, and sometimes an aggressive, desperate war for our appreciation, perhaps our affection. As a result he sometimes lost his sense of proportion and of good taste.

I remembered well that in a house of mourning it was forbidden to laugh and forbidden to say the word "shalom." In my eyes this prohibition had a very grave, almost magical, force, as if something terrible would happen if it were defied. I kept reminding myself of it all the time I sat there, so as not to say "shalom" automatically as I left the room. I was afraid that one of the others might slip up and say it. Silence fell again. It was very hot in the room and we sat without moving, our backs against the wall, waiting for rescue.

Suddenly Pesach's brother said: "Are there couples in your class already?"

Pesach burst out laughing. I wondered if he had forgotten that his mother was dead, allowing himself to burst out laughing like that, free of all restraint. His brother waited for a reply and stared at Rachel Hyman. He measured her from top to toe with great interest. Then he looked at Eli. He had noticed the connnection between them. Eli said: "Yes, there are couples."

The brother seemed gratified by this answer and Eli blushed.

Pesach said: "Those two are a couple," and he pointed at Rachel and Eli.

One of the old women wiped her tears on her sleeve and said: "You should only be healthy, and your parents should be healthy too."

Pesach's brother smiled at Rachel and there was something suspect in his smile. He opened his mouth to say something, but at that moment Eli stood up and we all followed suit. The mourners remained seated in their places and we made our way outside by ourselves. To my relief, none of us pronounced the word "shalom." We walked down the palm avenue and the air outside was refreshing after the stifling heat of the room. We reached the dirt road and Eli stopped for a moment and studied the big house as if he were trying to understand something which only accurate observation would be able to clarify. We walked on, waiting for Arik to say something. We needed him to say something now. But he knew it and kept quiet. Like a spoiled actor he waited for us to beg him, but we knew that in the end he wouldn't be able to restrain himself.

"What interests me," said Arik, "is where they hired those two wailing women of theirs and if they pay them by the day or by piecework, according to the amount they produce." And he immediately let out a squeaky, high-pitched wail and said: "You should only be healthy, and your parents should be healthy too, and your uncles and aunts and neighbors. . . ."

We all burst out laughing. We could never resist his imitations, which were the quintessence of absurdity and ugliness.

"Oh but you're mean," said Naomi, "you're so mean," but she herself writhed with laughter like the rest of us and her words only made us laugh even harder. We were laughing so much that we couldn't go on walking. We stepped off the road onto the hillside, leaned against a tree and waited to recover our composure, and then, exhausted, we sat down on the ground with our backs to the tree, surrounding it on all sides. Dusk was beginning to fall. On one side we could see the last houses of the town at the bottom of the hill, and on the other fields and citrus groves as far as the horizon. I told myself that I should keep this moment locked in my memory as a moment of grace. It was one of those rare moments when hidden barriers are breached and old grievances forgotten and time seems to stand still. We panted for breath, groaned, and said nothing. Each of us looked in front of him at his bit of the view, and not at the people sitting next to him, because our sense of being together was too strong to need any visual confirmation. Letting go had brought with it a wonderful feeling of friendship which I hoped would go on and on in order to stay strong in my memory for other hours and days to come. Naomi roused herself first:

"Did you see his brother? He seems like a big Don Juan."

"He seems to me like a sex maniac," said Rachel with a expression of prim revulsion on her face.

"I bet he is," said Arik. "He was looking at you all the time. He fancies you."

"Nonsense!" protested Rachel with a faint smile of satisfaction.

"I don't feel like going to the rehearsal now," said Eli. Perhaps he too didn't want it to end too soon. In the evening he had a rehearsal with the youth movement folk-dancing troupe. His daily schedule was packed with activities: as an athlete he had to train with the HaPoel youth team, and apart from being a counsellor in the youth movement, he also played the accordion and belonged to the folk-dancing troupe. After all this he even had time left to do his homework and read scientific books. He was an outstanding student. He always knew what he wanted and nothing could distract him from his path. Time obeyed his sense of order and inner discipline. Accordingly, when he said that he didn't feel like going to the rehearsal we knew that soon he would get up and go as planned, and he wouldn't let himself be carried away by a passing mood.

And indeed a few minutes later he stood up and shook the dust off his short trousers. He took a few steps, stopped for a moment and looked down at the town below us, and then looked behind him—at us. He took it for granted that we would get up and go with him.

When we arrived at the youth movement den it was already evening and the *hamsin* had lifted. Arik and I were the only ones in the group who weren't members of this youth movement—Arik had left it in the wake of a quarrel with Eli. Even after they were reconciled Arik didn't go back to the den, and he began to regard the whole business of the youth movement as phoney, ridiculous and childish. We went into the hut to see the folk-dancing rehearsal. Rachel and Eli went straight to the corner where the dancers were standing with their instructor, and the rest of us sat on a long wooden bench and looked at them. After a few minutes they cleared the benches from about half the area of the hut and made themselves a dance floor. They all took off their sandals and the boys took off their shirts and undershirts because it was hot inside. They paired off, the instructor beat the drum, and they began to dance. There was a dismissive smile in Arik's eyes as he looked at the dancers. He liked to say that these folk dances had nothing to do with dancing or folklore, but were artificial, ugly and ridiculous. He preferred, so he said, the authentic, popular folklore which stemmed from the ancient origins of the people, and not from the inventions of a few crazy kibbutzniks. But I found these dances beautiful with their subtle Oriental tunes and the longings for ancient times reflected in them. Thus, more or less, I pictured to myself the ancient Canaanite people, smelling of sweat and dust, like the smell now filling the air of the hut. The faces of the dancers were red and flushed and their bodies wet with sweat. Arik gestured to us from time to time in grotesque mimicry of the movements of the dancers, but Naomi, who was sitting next to him, had withdrawn into herself, her eyes fixed on Eli and Rachel, a couple in the troop as well. The blush spreading over her cheeks betrayed her thoughts. Eli cut a striking figure in the dance. His bare torso was bronzed and shining with sweat, and the sheen emphasized his athletic body, the curve of his muscles, his broad shoulders, his sturdy chest and narrow hips; all his movements bespoke suppleness, obedience to his will, they radiated strength and confidence. And Rachel was leaning on his arm like a tender flower, her hair very black, her face long and delicate and her eyes big and dark, slightly slanting, her figure slender, and her whole person softness and grace. Opposite this beauty Naomi felt her own poverty, and again she was seized by the desire to be wiped off the face of the earth—together with the pair of them. She was rather clumsy and short, her legs were thick, and locks of fair, untidy hair lay gracelessly on her forehead and nape. She loved him secretly with a stifled, suppressed, hopeless love and she struggled with herself never to let it be revealed. She wrote him poems and letters which she kept hidden in a locked drawer and she was sure that she would never know love, because she was under a kind of curse. She sought his closeness, always took part in activities where he was involved, but never crossed the line lest he find out. She was devoted to Eli and Rachel with all her heart, and they gave her their loyal friendship in return, liked her for her good sense, her honesty, her kind heart and her sensitivity. They admired her seriousness in everything she did. At parties and celebrations Naomi would read her favorite poems from books we did not know and which were not on the curriculum. We had no idea how personally she took these poems, how far she was expressing her own secret longings when she read them. Perhaps only Arik sensed it, for there existed between them a kind of unspoken understanding and mutual esteem which had grown up over many years of friendship and had not been disrupted by feelings in excess of that.

The dancers took a rest and Eli and Rachel came to sit next to us on the wooden bench, sweating and panting.

"He was making fun of the dancing all the time," said Rachel and smiled wearily. "You think I didn't see?"

"Me?!" Arick pretended to be astonished. "Where did you get that idea? It's great, really, I swear it is! Why don't you ever believe me? It's *really* great!" And he wrinkled his brow in his characteristic ironic frown and laid his hand on his heart, all injured innocence. "Go on," he turned to me, "tell them, did I make fun of the dancing?" He knew that if he asked Noami she would tell the truth. She was incapable of lying.

"I saw," said Rachel. "During the dance I looked at you and I saw you."

Eli said: "One day we'll drag you into the dance and force you to dance with everybody else, like everybody else, so that for once in your life you'll know how it feels not to be different, special, original, superior, cleverer than everybody else."

And so saying he gripped Arik by the neck as if he wanted to strangle him. Arik wriggled about and tried to free himself, but Eli laughed and wouldn't let him go. "Will you dance?" he asked. "Will you dance with everybody else?" Naomi looked at them with some concern. She knew that the beautiful can hurt without meaning to, even when they mean well, even when prompted by affection and friendship, but always out of the same careless, selfish superficiality. When Eli let go there were two reddish bruises on Arik's throat, but he pretended that it didn't hurt. He suffered from asthma, and Naomi was afraid that Eli's stranglehold would bring on a choking attack. We didn't know much about his illness. In my eyes it all seemed rather mysterious. Arik avoided talking about it and when I once asked him what it felt like to have an attack he didn't answer. It hardly ever happened in our presence; once or twice it happened in class and he went straight to the nurse's room, where he apparently received some kind of treatment, and then went home.

"Will you dance?" Eli repeated his question.

"You bet!" said Arik. "And how I'll dance!" He made an effort to smile. "After you see me dance you'll never want to dance again!"

The instructor called Eli and Rachel and they joined the other dancers. The rehearsal resumed. Now they danced a Russian folk dance and Rachel had another partner because Eli was standing in the center of the circle playing the accordion. It was the battered old accordion that belonged to the den, and Eli, accustomed to his own Emilio-Soprani, shook his head impatiently when it played a discord or when one of the sounds was blocked. He was absorbed in his playing, his head rolled backwards and we saw his prominent Adam's apple rising and falling as he breathed or swallowed his saliva.

When we emerged into the darkness a cool, pleasant breeze brushed our faces. We walked for a while without talking. I was overcome by the strange sadness I sometimes felt without knowing where it came from. A sense of the pointlessness of everything and not really belonging to anything. I wondered if they felt this too or if it was only my own defect, that every minute of happiness had to be paid for with hours of sadness. Everything around me seemed to be fading, dying, lost. The lighted houses, the people passing us in the street, my friends by my side, as if the supply of energy in nature had run out and the last effort to hang on had begun—a hopeless effort. And there was nothing to long for or really believe in. Was it because of this that they too were silent?

Eli and Rachel lengthened their stride and walked ahead. They exchanged a few words in whispers. When they had finished conferring Eli stopped and waited for us to catch up with them. He went up to Arik, put his arm around his shoulders and hugged him.

"Did I hurt you before?"

Arik protested: "Not a bit! It didn't hurt at all."

"So why are you sad? Rachel says I was out of line."

"I'm not sad. Do me a favor, Eli, don't start turning into my mother."

Arik extricated himself from Eli's embrace and began laughing loudly. I knew this forced, strained, artificial laugh of his. "Why are you so worried about me?" asked Arik. But Eli insisted on putting his arm around him again and said: "Sorry. I didn't mean to hurt you." This habit of Eli's of apologizing at every opportunity had been embarrassing us for years. He had a code of his own and there was no telling where it came from. He behaved according to his own rules without any shame, ignoring our rules which were self-evident and natural. I didn't always succeed in formulating his rules to myself when I puzzled over his behavior. We went on walking in silence.

Suddenly we heard the fire engine's siren behind us and a moment later it raced past and disappeared at the end of the road. The first *hamsin* days of spring always brought fires with them and to me they seemed like warning signals appearing in a different place every time, to warn of another, general, danger, immeasurably greater than that of the fires themselves. I didn't know what it was but I could sense it. I wasn't afraid of it, and it didn't even succeed in rousing me from the feeling of futility which often visited me at that time. After an hour or so the feeling would pass of its own accord, without, however, entirely disappearing, but remaining in the background like a dim, monotonous, distant buzzing. I knew that it was a hard time for me and I preferred not to understand it but to wait for it to come to an end. At moments like these I always wanted to be alone, but my will was so weak and my feet carried me forward with the others, aimlessly on and on. They had ceased to interest me and I was totally absorbed in myself. When I was with them my thoughts would drift. At home I would spend hours with the radio, trying to pick up remote stations on the short waves as if I might hear secret broadcasts there, directed at me by unknown forces. In the babble of whistles and growls, the voices alternately rising and falling and the strains of music and song bursting out and abruptly stifled I discovered a cruel and elusive world. There were vast spaces of silence and then dozens of voices all clustered round one point on the frequency band, clinging to each other with blind fanaticism, fighting for their place with all their might, trying to wear one another out, to drown out all the other voices, to prevail, conquer and rule. It was clear to me that this specific tiny point on the frequency band had been chosen completely randomly and it had no advantages over the infinite number of empty points in the silent spaces around it, which could easily have accommodated each and every one of the voices. But they all crowded stubbornly round the same one point. I understood that it wasn't the point they were fighting for but their lives, and that they had no lives except in a place they had to fight for until they killed themselves. Because from the moment one of the voices prevailed over its opponents and announced its victory clearly, loudly and arrogantly, you could rest assured that its day was done and that it would soon begin to fade and another voice would gather force, rise above it and drive it out. These creatures from other worlds, they spoke in tongues and noises I was not familiar with and tunes I had never heard in my life. Once in a while a familiar tune would make itself heard in the tumult of the war and I knew that someone from our world was also there, but I felt no preference, no special sympathy or identification, and no wish for him to win. The principle and pattern of this war interested me more than its outcome for one of the participants. I believed that all radios picked up different combinations of short-wave transmissions according to the scale of the intervals on their frequency bands and that therefore the signals which I picked up were unique to me, presenting me with possibilities that I didn't yet know how to decipher but which were full of significance. My parents couldn't understand what I was doing huddled up next to the radio and disapproved of me wasting my time in this way. When they addressed me, or asked me what station I was looking for, I would be as startled as if I were suddenly waking from a deep trance, so far had I receded into myself and so detached was I from the outside world.

On the other hand, I experienced bursts of energy and curiosity. At such times my friends attained great importance in my eyes. I would try to guess their innermost thoughts, to pinpoint the difference between what was really going on inside them and the show they put on for the outside world. (I didn't yet understand that the social display was no less true than the hidden thought and that both expressed in different ways, as in two different languages, the very same thing.) The moments when I took an interest in my friends and tried to read their thoughts gave me a feeling of liberation and power, as if I had somehow entrenched myself within them, whether they liked it or not, in a spot that belonged exclusively to me. When I withdrew into myself, however, I imagined that I was renouncing everything for something very great. Sometimes I would be enjoyably caught in the soft threads of an infinite web, sinking into a dream full of images of love and lapped in the moist, benevolent warmth of death. Each of my friends knew more or less what he wanted to be in the future, or so I assumed, whereas I still clung to the remnants of fantasies and ancient longings.

A week later Pesach came back to school, sat down at his desk, and when the English lesson began he no longer shrank into his corner with his head hunched between his shoulders as if he wanted to disappear or merge into the wall, but raised his head and looked defiantly straight into teacher Benno's eyes. There was a new, more confident expression on his face. Benno noticed him immediately after his long absence and his eyes already held the sweet, ironic and insulting smile which he always had ready for Pesach.

"Welcome back, Pesach!" cried Benno. "We missed you last week. We wanted to hear your analysis of Shelley's 'Ode to the West Wind' which we studied here and there was nobody to take your place. Now that you're here we can relax. *If Winter comes, can Spring be far behind?*"

Benno surveyed the room, waiting for the laughter which usually greeted his sallies at Pesach's expense. But a wall of silence confronted him.

He was a relatively young teacher, an immigrant from one of the East European countries. He had the reputation of being a skirt-chaser and heartbreaker. For a time all the girls in the class had been in love with him except for the one whom he apparently really loved, Rachel Hyman. She claimed that he was "slimy and disgusting." He was tall, with a bony face that was tanned all year round, as if he spent the winters skiing, and pale, supercilious steel-cold eyes. His nostrils always quivered sensuously, as if they smelled scents on the air that we were too young and ignorant to know.

Pesach sat at his ease and smiled. Benno looked alternately at Pesach and at the class and a cloud of anxiety descended on him. The silence continued. He shot us an inquiring look, as if to ask: What's wrong? For a moment he seemed at a loss, but he immediately recovered, returned to the platform, looked at us again with an expression of revulsion and disdain, and became brisk and businesslike. He instructed us to open our books at a certain page, sat down, read Wordsworth's poem about the daffodils and explained it. He went on talking for a long time like this, as if he wanted to be alone with English poetry and avoid any exchanges with us. But he sensed the whispers, the hostile looks and the smell of rebellion in the air. He stood up and surveyed us again from the platform. He no longer wore the proud, disdainful expression. His face was calm and concentrated.

Naomi sent a note to Eli. Her face was red with anger and emotion. Arik mumbled some joke and the noise of the whispering grew louder.

Benno seemed to have come to a decision. He stepped off the platform and went up to Eli's desk: "Perhaps you'd like to tell me what all these whispers and consultations are about? It's impossible to continue with the lesson like this."

Eli whispered something into Benno's ear and the teacher said:

"I didn't know. After the lesson I'll invite him to the staff room and apologize."

"No," said Eli, "in front of the whole class, just like you hurt his feelings in front of everybody."

Benno's steely eyes opened wide in anger: "No! I don't ask you how to behave and you don't give me orders."

He returned to his platform. "Pesach, after the lesson come and see me in the staff room," he said dryly and thought that this concluded the episode. He returned to the English poem.

During recess it was decided to declare a strike until the English teacher apologized to Pesach in front of the class. Eli went up to Pesach and asked him not to go to the staff room. But Pesach was unmoved by the storm raging around him. He sat confidently in his place smiling his new smile to which we were not yet accustomed and said: "I don't care what he said and I don't know what you want."

"For him to know that there's a limit to his nerve," Naomi seethed, "that there are some things he can't do."

"He probably didn't know," said Pesach. "What's there to make such a fuss about? He always talks to me like that. It goes in one ear and out the other. Do me a favor and leave it alone."

He spoke confidently and there was strength in the expression on his face. As if he understood our motives better than we understood them ourselves, as if he sensed that our wish to confront the English teacher and try to humiliate him was more important to us than the insult to Pesach. But we paid no attention to what he said. Even after he went to the staff room and returned after a while and went back to his corner—we stood by our decision to strike. The headmaster tried to persuade the class committee to see the English teacher's apology to Pesach as the end of the incident. But Eli stood his ground and we stood behind him.

The next lesson was due to begin and we gathered in the grove of trees on the school grounds, refusing to go into the classroom.

The spirit of rebellion and the danger sent a nervous frisson of pleasure through us. The fear of the consequences of our action brought us together, as if it was too much for the individual to cope with, and therefore we had to draw strength from each other and the spirit of unity. Arik stood leaning against a tree, his hands in his pockets, grinning. He too had been infected by the feverish glee. But above all he was glad of the opportunity to see us all in a state of hysterical excitement. There was something in his smile which said: It's an old story, we've seen it all before and we know how it ends.

One of the students cried: "Where's Pesach?"

Pesach wasn't with us. Eli's eyes searched for him among us and didn't find him. Eli's forehead creased in the stern, angry frown which is often to be seen in the portraits of great revolutionaries and fighters for justice and freedom. "He must have stayed in the classroom, the idiot," he muttered. He went to look for him. We remained in the grove, absorbed in our affairs.

Eli entered the classroom and saw Pesach sitting in his place, his face on his hands and his elbows on the desk, his eyes half-asleep.

"Why aren't you with everybody?" asked Eli.

"I don't want to," replied Pesach.

"But we're doing it all for you," protested Eli.

"Don't do me any favors! I'm not interested," said Pesach. "I told you to leave it alone."

Eli approached him, put a friendly hand on his arm and tried to pull him up.

"Don't touch me!" said Pesach and leaped to his feet. "You want a fight?"

Eli was astounded. And before he could find anything to say Pesach quickly took off his shirt and jumped him, seizing him by the shoulders and trying to push him to the ground. Eli tried to slip out of his grasp but the grip was too strong. A couple of punches to the stomach led Eli to lose his famous self-control and his Olympian calm. He began to fight back. But it was a hard fight, and he couldn't beat Pesach. When we came into the classroom to look for Eli we found them locked together, writhing on the floor, puffing and panting and wet with sweat. A few of the students tried to separate them straightaway, but Eli called out in a strangled, high-pitched voice: "Don't interfere, I'll finish him off." We'd never heard Eli speak in such a strange voice before.

We surrounded them in a circle and watched the fight. In contrast to other fights which we accompanied by comments and laughter and cheers from the onlookers, this time we stood and looked in silence, as if something fateful was about to be decided, something that affected us all. The sound of their heavy breathing and the thudding of their bodies on the floor filled the room. Eli strained himself to the utmost but met his match in Pesach, who remained as taut as a spring, unflagging, his muscles swelling and his back broad and supple, his movements coordinated and powerful. Drops of sweat dripped from the red hair in his armpits.

Eli's strength failed him. Pesach knocked him to the ground, stood up and breathed deeply. His chest swelled and shrank to the rhythm of his breathing, high and broad, and a slender stripe of yellowish fuzz ran down its center, from the bottom of his throat to his waist. He raised his head and looked at us. I had never seen his eyes so green, staring at us quietly and cruelly. This was no longer the bedraggled cat we had once known. Before there had seemed to be something oppressing his natural form from outside, preventing it from filling out, marring it, slackening its lines and blurring it until it seemed amorphous, and now the inner form had woken up, prevailed, and imposed its lines on the outside. He stood with his prey at his feet, like a savage young animal, everything about him coordinated and erect, to the bristles of red hair on his head, smiling calmly, contemptuous of any possible threat, without satisfaction or surprise at his victory, without curiosity about its effect on us, without any emotion at all. I knew that all those standing around me were sensible of the strange, unexpected beauty which had been revealed to us. I saw it in the blushes of embarrassment and fear on the cheeks of the girls, transfixed by the wild animal which had burst its bars, and in the eyes of the boys, filled with restlessness and mortification by feelings they did not know existed. But I had always loved the beauty of the vanquished, the stunned looks on their faces, as if they had been hypnotized or held in thrall by a strange, seductive spell, the weeping of the defeated, submissive body, the moan of strangled helplessness escaping their lips, their heartbreak at the betrayal of their bodies and their trampled pride. Accordingly, I didn't take my eyes off Eli, who was helped up by Arik and resisted his help, looking around him with narrowed eyes, as if waking from a deep sleep, stretching his neck and arms, his face suddenly contorted, unable to suppress the expression of pain and sorrow. His eyes rested on Pesach standing opposite him, smiling with green eyes, staring like the eyes of a wild cat, and then he did something that only Eli with his unique code of behavior was capable of doing: he went up to Pesach and offered him his hand to shake. Pesach immediately stiffened, ready to jump in case Eli was trying to deceive him with some clever trick. He quickly parted his legs to steady his stance, thrust his torso forward, examined Eli's face suspiciously, and finally held out a hesitant hand from a safe distance.

Eli went outside to the water fountain to wash his face. We knew that he wanted to be alone and nobody accompanied him. Not even Rachel, who sat down at her desk in the classroom, looking pensive, her face not revealing her thoughts. Eli bent over the basin of the water fountain, cupped the water in his hands and splashed it on his face with great force, almost furiously, almost in self-hatred, as if he wanted to punish himself for his sins and was about to flagellate himself. He lashed water onto his face without stopping. His blue eyes reddened at the contact with the water as if they were crying, and the streams pouring down his cheeks looked like giant tears. He shut off the tap, stood still and let the water flow down his neck, his shoulders and the white undershirt peeping out of his shirt which had been torn in the fight. He stood and concentrated for a moment. The yard was deserted, everyone was back in class. He closed his eyes, trying to remember if anything like this had ever happened to him before. When? Why did he have such a strong feeling that all this had already happened once, that he himself had already experienced it, detail by detail; perhaps in the days of his most distant childhood, perhaps in a forgotten dream, perhaps in another dimension of time?

When he returned to the classroom we were all sitting in our places and the headmaster and homeroom teacher were getting ready to haul us over the coals. When the headmaster saw Eli coming into the room, his shirt torn and water dripping from him, he cried in alarm: "What's the meaning of this?" Eli stood in the doorway, his eyes downcast, and said nothing. He walked slowly to his desk, took his things, made his way calmly and erectly between the desks, and without giving anyone so much as a glance left the room.

Pesach stared at the window. The signs of the fight were no longer evident on him. All this was none of his concern. His elbow was on the desk, his chin resting on his hand and his eyes waiting for something to happen in the courtyard he could see out of the window. His forehead would crease for a moment as if he were making an effort to think or focusing his vision on something, and then his face would immediately clear again.

During that summer the mask of dark freckles vanished gradually from his face, as if dislodged and dispersed by some inner power breaking through, and a new, unfamiliar face appeared beneath it. At first the green eyes, which had once been two colorless slits, opened, and a wild animal which knew no law but its own appetite and freedom looked out. At first the look was still suspicious, hesitant, evading contact, wary of traps, taking the measure of the alien land as if haunted by the memory of a previous imprisonment. His eyebrows and eyelashes which had once been very fair and indistingishable from the rest of his face now began to darken and cast a shadow of mystery over his eyes. And then the dread of imprisonment and shrinking from contact gave way to a challenge to anyone who dared to cross the border of the forbidden circle. And under the disintegrating net of freckles the high cheekbones were exposed, endowing the face with restrained tension and arrogance, and the lips appeared, thick, fleshy and sensual. The bristles of ginger hair which always stuck out untidily on his head and forehead grew into a reddish mop through which he would sometimes slowly run his fingers with a dreamy, self-absorbed expression, or push away the unruly curl which always fell over his forehead and touched his left eyebrow, tossing his head as he did so in a gesture of clumsy vanity. He spoke little, and had no friends in the class apart from a few nonentitites with whom he sometimes played football in the school yard. They were in awe of him and looked up to him because he was a few years older than they were, and also because they had seen him get the better of Eli Shapira; but he showed no affection toward them whatsoever.

We didn't know yet how to behave toward him. By winter there was hardly a trace of the old cloddish presence which had been the butt of our jokes and humiliations for years, and we had not yet grown accustomed to the new one. If he had been a new student it would have been easier to befriend him, but whenever we looked at Pesach we always imagined his old shadow limping along a few steps behind him, transparent and ingratiating. Until we noticed that the prettiest girls in the class were vying for his attention.

If beauty is the symmetry of limbs and stature, the correct proportion of every detail in its relation to other details, the aesthetic harmony of the color of eyes, hair and skin, then this description fit Eli Shapira. Eli's beauty was comprehensible. If he hadn't already begun to shave his face, its shape and complexion would have been like that of a beautiful girl's face, with Eli's black hair and blue eyes, slender well-drawn eyebrows, and long black eyelashes which lent a reflective softness to his look. And his body was molded according to all the laws of beauty and harmonious proportions, tall, athletic and well-developed. But if beauty is that mysterious inner radiance which we see reflected in the look of the eyes, the expression of the face, the posture and movements of the body, in all of these together plus something else which has no name but which sets its stamp on the whole and gives the onlooker a sense of danger—then there was beauty in Pesach's new incarnation. But I found it difficult to account for this new beauty even though I felt its presence. It was foreign to my ideas. I couldn't understand what it was that made the girls of the class, even the prettiest of them, direct looks of yearning veiled with self-righteous resentment at Pesach, who walked among them as an uninvited guest, an intruder, a provocateur. He looked like an emissary from a distant and hostile, dark and barbaric land. The looks and whispers, the hostility and embarrassment to which Pesach gave rise in their hearts, roused me to make an effort to understand the nature of this beauty, which was obscure to me. But the only conclusion to which my efforts led me was that in contrast to the calm and trust inspired by the figure of Eli, Pesach gave rise to a sense of uncertainty and danger.

One day somebody in class said that he had seen Pesach screwing Nehama the prostitute in the cemetery at midnight. The cemetery was always the nocturnal setting chosen for such stories. I knew that there was no truth at all in the tale, but for some reason, in spite of myself, the scene appeared in my imagination in a very convincing light. It fit in with the way I now saw Pesach. I imagined him and Nehama the prostitute dancing naked in the moonlight among the gravestones. It was easy for me to believe anything weird and unhealthy in connection with Pesach. The stories and jokes multiplied. Arik's skits were full of hints and grotesque witticisms about Pesach's love affairs, which made us rock with laughter. But Pesach didn't laugh. He sat indifferently as they were read out during the cultural program at our Friday homeroom socials. At first Arik took care not to mention Pesach's name in these skits, because there was no knowing how the wild cat might react, sitting in his corner in a disturbing silence, with only his jaw muscles moving rhythmically, like the throbbing of a mechanism ready to spring into action, as if he were sharpening his teeth. Little by little the hints became more explicit, gleeful and defiant. As far as Arik was concerned there was nothing that wasn't a joking matter, and nothing, it seemed, was hidden from his eyes. Eli said to him: "Be careful, he's psychologically disturbed, he's not sane and he's capable of anything." But Arik was beyond reason. The image of Eli lying defeated on the class floor in front of everybody would not leave him be, even after two months. The burning insult marred his wit. He was no longer an observer from the side, his humor was sometimes crude and forced. He lay in wait for Pesach's every movement, for every word that broke his sleepy silence.

The light was on in the classroom because it had suddenly grown dark outside and the sky was charged with black clouds. I loved these moments before the deluge and the misleading softness in which they steeped the atmosphere of the room. I looked round at my friends to see the effect of the light on them. There was a stir round Arik's desk. I imagined he had made some wisecrack. He himself bit his lips to hold back his laughter, and his whole chest shuddered with the effort. He motioned to me to look at Pesach. I looked behind me and saw him sitting at his desk with nothing out of the way about him. The rumor passed from desk to desk. I saw the girls blushing and hiding their faces in their hands and the boys grinning in enjoyment and embarrassment. The literature teacher, who was new, a pleasant young woman whom we all liked, sensed that attention was being directed toward some point in the back of the class. She asked for quiet and attention, but instead her request released the laughter which everyone had been trying to hold in. The possibility of her being brought face to face with what had happened to Pesach was sensationally funny and thrilling. The literature teacher was not used to being treated by us in this fashion: she filled with insult and anger, and seeing that all eyes were directed at Pesach, she concluded that he had played some trick or said something to make everybody laugh. She went up to his desk and asked him to leave the room.

Pesach remained seated for a moment, considering his options. "Didn't you hear me?" cried the literature teacher. "I told you to leave the room!" He looked at us. I imagined I could see contempt on his face. He plucked up the courage to stand up. When he stood I saw what my friends had seen from the side and I hadn't seen because the desk hid half his body from me: a prominent swelling in the front of his trousers. He twisted his face into an expression of sorrow and resignation and walked down the aisle between the desks. But as he passed Arik's desk he stopped for a moment and smiled defiantly as if to say: There, look to your heart's content, I don't care. The literature teacher, who had discovered the cause of the laughter, was overcome by confusion and said to Pesach before he left the room: "They'll get over their silly laughter in a minute. Wait outside for five minutes and then come back. All right?"

She concluded with a question in order to soften the severity of the punishment. But Pesach didn't answer her. He was already outside, in his natural territory. After a moment I saw him from my desk, through the window, in the empty school yard, under a sky as black as lead, kicking an old tin can, playing football with himself.

At the end of the lesson Pesach returned to the classroom with the swelling in his trousers gone. He went up to Arik, who immediately recoiled in a defensive movement. But Pesach reassured him: "Don't be afraid. I don't want to hit you, because you're weak. But if you're so brainy and you're as clever as you think you are, why did you show it to the girls too? Are you crazy? What kind of a guy are you?"

Pesach's argument was well received by his audience, including those who had enjoyed themselves and had a good laugh in the literature lesson, and even Eli said to Arik: "This time you went too far." And again Arik felt that everyone was against him, he wasn't adjusting himself quickly enough to the changes, and there was no connection between what he did and what happened to him. And without approval and confirmation and affection Arik felt lonely and lost. He forced his face into the strained smile which I didn't like seeing there, in order to hide his unhappiness. Afterward we walked home from school together, because Eli went to train at HaPoel.

Arik said: "A lot of people say you should be happy when you're young, it's the best time of your life, you'll always look back with longing to those days. But I know they're being hypocritical when they say it. I'll never long for these days. We're like slaves.

We have to do what we're told, eveybody tries to influence us, to educate us, to unload something on us. Why can't they just leave us alone, to be what we really are? Remember what I'm telling you: I'll never long for these days. I want to be free and do the most terrible things with nobody to tell me if it's good or bad, and the responsibility will be mine."

I said to him: "Maybe we're not whole people yet, maybe there's still something lacking in us, some strength or special kind of intelligence, to fit us for freedom and independence?"

"On the contrary!" cried Arik. "You know that according to science man reaches the height of his development at our age? Until the age of eighteen, twenty maximum. It could be a wonderful age, if only they let us live it in the right way. But by the time we can live the way we want to, we'll already have begun the slow process of aging that lasts until we die. After the age of twenty the body loses strength every day, the brain decays and gradually shrinks."

I smiled. I thought that this was another one of his jokes. But he stood his ground. He had never spoken to me so seriously. Never before had I felt so strongly his willingness to speak to me with this sort of frankness, because he had always considered me childish. "Don't laugh," he said, "this is a fact known to every biologist today. Ask Eli. We both read it in a scientific magazine his father gets from America. If you like, Eli can show it to you."

Nothing like this had ever occurred to me before. I lived in the feeling that everything was still before me and all I had to do was get through this miserable period. Nothing was fixed, nothing was spoiled yet, and it was still possible to let my thoughts dwell on hopes, fantasies, daydreams, until the moment of truth of my call-up arrived. And now it transpired that precisely then the terrible process of aging and decay began. Was this why Arik was so cynical? Perhaps it was the reason for his despair (I had never doubted that he knew despair better than any of us and hid it from us; perhaps this was his great secret). He knew better than we did the terrible waste of our lives at their prime. I examined Arik's face and it seemed to me that the fatal process of aging had already begun to show its signs. Perhaps because he had found out about it prematurely, illegitimately, without permission, and now some god was taking revenge for his exaggerated curiosity. There was a disagreeable sourness on his face, his narrow lips expressed a hidden pain, and his eyes, since the steady flow of wit and flashing malice had ceased, looked dead behind his glasses.

"You mean," I tried to refute this theory, "that after the age of eighteen you actually begin to die?"

"Of course!" cried Arik impatiently, as if I had just understood, "What did you think? That natural death was a sudden event, an accident that happens to a person in old age? That's the way it is in movies and novels but not in real life. According to the discoveries of modern science the whole of life after youth is a slow death. Every minute more and more cells in your body die and more and more parts of your brain decay and go to sleep forever. A man grows weaker and weaker from both the physical and mental point of view."

It was evident that Arik derived a peculiar enjoyment from frightening me with this theory and that he was deliberately exaggerating. We reached the crossroads and the sky was still like a black dome over our heads, close to bursting. But I wanted to go on talking to him. It wasn't often that I had the opportunity to talk to him seriously. I saw that he too wanted the conversation to continue. Perhaps because his pride had been wounded in the classroom and especially because Eli had been among those who agreed with Pesach's accusation and said: "This time you've gone too far." We sat down on the curb, set our satchels down beside us, and for a moment he was silent. I tried again to refute his theory: "If all that's correct and it's so famous and the only ones who don't know about it are the young people themselves, then that means the whole adult world is keeping it a secret from them, on purpose. . . ."

"And when we find out—it will be too late, death will already be within us and we'll carry on with it inside us and get older and older and keep it a secret from the young generation after us? Yes! Exactly! And you know that the years between adolescence and twenty are the years of our greatest sexual capacity too? But society is built so that we're regarded as babies from the sexual point of view. We're not prepared for it in time, there's no framework of sexual activity for young people. On the contrary, it's considered a scandal, a deviation, a crime."

"So there's nothing worth believing in, aspiring to, dreaming about?" I asked.

"The only thing worth aspiring to," said Arik, "is reaching the peak. But when you're already there and you can't enjoy it and take advantage of it because you're like a slave and all that awaits you is deterioration and decay, what is there to hope for or dream about? Don't you understand? We're at the peak now, at our maximum, and we can't do anything with it, because we're chained up like slaves in a cave, without seeing the true light of outside, and living with shadows."

"So how are you going to live your life?" I asked. I was always sure that Arik had a clear goal and definite plans for his future.

"As soon as I feel that I'm beginning to age, I'll kill myself," he said without pathos, in a dry, businesslike, matter-of-fact tone. "But the trouble is that when the time comes, because of the weakness and stupidity that will have already begun to get a grip on me, I may not have the courage or the intelligence to understand what's really happening to me and to do the right thing. And I'll sink into it just like everybody else. This will be my real test and I hope that in spite of everything I'll pass it. If I believed in God, I would ask him only one favor: to preserve my wits at that moment. But I don't believe in God. So I have to remember always the things that I understand now and not allow time and weakness to change my mind."

"Do your parents know about it?"

I knew that this question would immediately betray the childishness which Arik always mocked. But I was only trying to see his decision in concrete terms, in the context of his actual life; everything stopped being clearcut when I pictured Arik to myself in his natural setting, i.e., his family, the world of other people. I knew his parents. They were much older than mine; (perhaps the dread of old age came to him from his life with them) and they spoiled him because of his gifts and his illness. I tried to relate them to his fateful decision and put the contemplated deed to the test of concrete reality. This thought gave me pain and a strange sense of guilt, whose cause I only understood on the evening of the same day. I was sorry I had asked the question. But Arik didn't laugh at my childish question, he only gave me a look of despair, regretting the effort he had wasted in vain on trying to open my eyes to the truth.

"What's it got to do with my parents?" he asked me sullenly as if I had thrust a responsibility upon him which he was unwilling to accept. "Do I tell them how to live? Did I choose them to be my parents? It's only an accident that I'm their son. True, I love them because I've lived with them from the day I was born and they sacrificed a lot for me, but this love isn't a moral virtue but my weakness. True love must be chosen, conquered, suffered, and not received ready-made. And this isn't my only weakness. I have weaknessness, I don't deny it. But I have no reason to be proud of them. I have fears, I know they're not logical, but that doesn't help me to get rid of them, they're stronger than I am. When my parents die it will be terribly painful for me. Of course, if I don't kill myself first, and I hope I will. But this pain isn't logical. Every day they die a little more, every day I say good-bye to another part of them that will never exist again. But the last minute will be hard, because from the emotional point of view a big part of me will die with them. So what? Should I let that change my way of life?"

"And does Eli know about your decision?" I asked. I knew he was the only person who had any influence over Arik.

"Yes, Eli knows," said Arik throughtfully and fell silent. Then he added: "Eli isn't what he once was. But he's still worth more than all the rest."

It was late. We stood up to go our separate ways. I felt very tired. I had a lot to digest. Not so much Arik's opinions and theories, but the special state of mind which had just been revealed to me and how to reconcile this with the person I had known for so many years. I had often wondered about his secret. I sensed that he had a secret, like everybody else. This secret, like a faithful demon, accompanies us all, protects us and guides our steps, and we repay it by our obedience and by hiding it inside us. This secret, I felt, makes each of us unique and sometimes incomprehensible. So, what was his secret? I didn't like Arik. I didn't like his arrogance, his absolute conviction of his own cleverness and his tendency to look down on others, even though I didn't doubt his intelligence and knowledge which far exceeded anything I had ever known. I didn't know what he thought of me and it was important to me to know. He didn't allow me to delude myself with false hopes:

"You're awfully childish, I bet you didn't understand a word I said," and the amused, cynical expression returned to his face. Perhaps he had decided to make things easier for me by reassuming at the end the role in which I was accustomed to seeing him; or perhaps he was afraid he had revealed too much and hurried to pay his dues to his secret demon. We said good-bye and he turned to the left. Before I contined on my way home I studied him from behind and there was no doubt in my mind: the slow death was already gnawing at him. He walked like someone not in control of his body, dragging his feet, his back stooped, his head hanging, his satchel dangling from his right hand as if it was about to slip out of his grasp and fall to the ground at any minute, his left hand in his trouser pocket. This is how his figure became etched in my memory. This is how I most vividly remember him now.

A moment later there was an explosion in the sky and the rain burst forth. It fell on me not far from my house, but by the time I arrived I was wet through. There was something threatening in this explosion of nature; there was no thunder or lightning but the downpour was so thick and heavy and it hit the ground with such force that I imagined I could hear the inner rumbling which is supposed to accompany earthquakes. The panic that seized hold of me, my flight and the drenched state in which I arrived home helped me shake off the disturbing impression left by my conversation with Arik, from which I tried to distract my thoughts. But that evening, when I was sitting at the supper table with my parents, another storm broke out with thunder and lightning and the electric lights went out in the house. My mother put an oil lamp which was kept in the cupboard for such occasions on the table. My parents' faces filled with shadows and suddenly the things Arik had said about his parents' slow death welled up in me and choked my throat. It was no longer the selfish fear of the death of my parents which would leave me alone, the fear which had horrified me as a child, but a sorrow, too heavy to bear, that I could do nothing to save them. I had never thought of them as old. They had always seemed ageless to me. But now the shadows of the oil lamp gnawing at their faces and throats, gouging big holes in them and distorting them beyond recognition, marked them with the fateful signs. Old age in all its horror was upon them. I knew that if it wasn't for their unwillingness to cause me pain, they would scream out loud. But they sat in silence, hostages to a cruel, hidden fate, forgiving as always my weakness and selfishness, waiting in patient resignation for the sentence to be carried out. Now I thought I understood what Arik had said about his parents dying a little every day and how every day he said good-bye to another part of them that would never exist again. They began to talk to each other but I didn't hear what they said, I knew that they were putting on an act for my sake, pretending that nothing had happened, that everything was as usual, in order to spare me sorrow and to reassure me that nothing was expected of me. This only increased my pain at my helplessness. I knew very well that I was torturing myself with a mirage, and that in a little while the light would go on and the nightmare would stop, but I was no longer certain that what I would see when the light went on would be more true than what I saw now. I felt a strong need to cry. It was so long since this need had visited me, I had forgotten what it felt like. And now it erupted like a convulsion from the pit of my stomach, flooding my chest and throat, and I didn't know how to stop it. I felt that I had to fight it with all my might until the electricity came back on. I tried to divert my mind with various thoughts, repeating to myself that it was only by accident that they were my parents, and they were only two strangers, I didn't choose them, but my heart knew that this accident was the accident of my life, and that I chose them every minute of every hour, consciously or unconsciously, that I clung to these two shadows and I would not be able to let go of them. At this minute my little brother called from his room and burst out crying. Perhaps he was terrified by the dark. There was always a little light shining in the passage all night long and he was used to its faint glow. The electricity failure had made his room dark. I quickly picked up the oil lamp and said that I would go and see what the matter was. As soon as I went out of the room I felt a sense of relief. I approached my brother's bed and a wave of love engulfed me. I bent over him and he stopped crying, looked at me for a minute as if he didn't know who I was, closed his eyes, and went back to sleep. I went on standing for a minute in his room, which was full of the special smell of his sleep; I loved this smell and I breathed it into my lungs. The oppressive feeling didn't go away, but sank back again to where it had come from, no doubt to wait there for another opportunity.

When I returned to the room, my mother said: "He must have had a bad dream." And the lights came on in the house.

At the end of the term Pesach was summoned to the headmaster's office and told that if he didn't make any progress in his studies he would not be able to sit for the examinations and there would be no point in his continuing presence in the classroom. A number of the best students in the class immediately volunteered to help him catch up. He didn't ask anyone for help, and perhaps he even found it burdensome and would have preferred to do without it, but the tide of interest and goodwill flowing from all sides was irresistible. In the afternoon the volunteers stayed behind at school to do his homework with him and explain whatever he didn't understand. Eli Shapira, who undertook to teach him mathematics, even claimed that he "wasn't stupid at all." One of the girls, whose parents came from America, tried to teach him English. Arik, the only one not swept up on the tide of enthusiasm, said: "It's just plain hypocrisy. It won't help. He's not cut out for study. I can understand why the girls are so keen to stay behind alone with him in the afternoons," he sniggered, "but the boys? He's an animal."

"That's not true, Arik," protested Naomi. "He's a nice boy but he's got problems and we have to help him. He's already much more sociable than he used to be and we have to make an effort to be friendly."

I saw in Pesach's eyes that all this made him uncomfortable. The affection and popularity that suddenly surrounded him disturbed him no less than the teasing and insults that were once his lot, and certainly more than the indifference and oblivion that followed them. But just as he had known how to submit to the insults in silence, he resigned himself to the new regime too. Some instinct, however, apparently told him that it was more dangerous now. He smiled and talked more than he used to, the smile exposed rows of yellowish teeth and his green eyes flashed with a strange, cold light. The girls saw these things as signs of friendliness and goodwill. When one of them sat in the classroom with him in the afternoon she usually brought a friend with her, "to stop people gossiping." But people gossiped anyway, and there was no knowing what was true and what was fiction. All the girls went about full of secrecy and mystery as if they knew something about Pesach that none of their friends knew. I watched him and saw how his confidence was crumbling, how the forbidden circle which had once guarded him so jealously was weakening and narrowing, and he was shrinking into his corner. Arik too saw this:

"They're trying to tame a wild animal," he said, "and there are three possibilities. Either it will give in, become domesticated, grow accustomed to its cage and lose all its natural strength; or it will break and die after a short time, because it won't be able to get used to living in a cage; or it will attack its tamers one day and eat them alive."

"And which of the three do you think will happen?"

"The first," said Arik to my surprise, "is the worst from his point of view and in my opinion it's what everyone wants."

"I thought you would go for the third possibility," I said.

"I wish!" Arik smiled in enjoyment as he pictured it.

Eli didn't agree with Arik. Their friendship seemed to be losing its bloom. Eli was always criticizing him: "You always have to be different, special, original. It's a childish desire to attract attention, it's the result of a refusal to accept reality."

"I think I see reality more clearly than you do," said Arik, "but the main thing is that I'm true to myself."

"Rubbish," said Eli angrily. "You always look for ulterior motives and sinister designs in everything and you can never take things simply for what they are."

They were standing next to the billboard opposite Eli's house, waiting for Rachel who was having a piano lesson; Arik took advantage of her absence to speak to his friend with complete frankness, as they had done in the past.

"We're not friends like we used to be," said Arik sadly.

"But nothing's like it used to be, don't you understand, Arik? Everything changes quickly, and new things enter the picture."

"Once you valued my opinion much more highly and it was important to you to hear it; now you object automatically to everything I say. Sometimes I think that you're afraid that if you agree with me you'll lose your independence; as if you hate me."

"That's not true!" protested Eli indignantly. "But when I don't agree with you I say so. What do you want? You want me to agree with everything you say for the sake of our friendship?"

"Everything got spoiled after that one quarrel," said Arik, "it all began from some bit of nonsense that you blew up out of all proportion."

"You behaved in an ugly way, Arik, you said things you shouldn't have said, and you admitted it yourself when you came to apologize and make up."

"One day you'll understand that it was Rachel who made trouble between us out of jealousy."

"Are you starting on that again?" said Eli in a threatening tone. "If anybody was jealous it wasn't Rachel."

"She couldn't stand the friendship between us, she felt excluded and she decided to destroy it."

"That's not true, she likes you a lot better than you think."

"You don't like me any more."

"Why are you talking nonsense? You're behaving like a spoiled child. You want everything for yourself. All the attention, all the affection, all the admiration. You're not willing to share it with anyone else. What you don't understand is that there are things outside friendship, things stronger than friendship. Things that are elemental, you can't fight them, it's a lost battle. All you can do is cooperate with them, exploit their energy, turn them from enemies to partners—or fight them and be crushed. It's a lost battle, Arik, you're fighting a lost battle. And when you begin to understand this, you get nervous, hysterical. The same thing goes for Pesach. Why does it bother you so much if I help him and try to befriend him? Is it at your expense? At the expense of our friendship? What are you afraid of?"

"Once we thought that our friendship would be above everything else," said Arik bitterly, "you believed that too."

"For God's sake," said Eli, "stop clinging to those childish ideas. What do you mean—above everything else? As if there was some sort of hierarchy. But why should one thing be at the expense of the other, above the other? I want love and friendship and I want to get on in life and I want to contribute to the state and society and it's all on the same level of importance for me. Anyone who devotes himself to one thing only goes mad in the end. It's only the correct balance and combination among them all that helps to realize each one of them. You still haven't accepted the relationship between Rachel and me. So get it into your head: I love Rachel and she's very important to me and I intend making her part of my life. And being my friend means being her friend too. And when you too have a girlfriend that you love, I'll do the same for you, and perhaps then you'll understand it better too. I don't know why—but you don't want to grow up, it's as if you want your childhood to go on forever with all its oaths of loyalty, its rituals. But for me it's over. What interests me is the future, I'm not interested in the old games any more. You'd better start learning to live with the new facts."

"Is there anything else you've got against me?"

"That's one of the old games too. I don't know why you're always trying to draw me into it. Okay. I'll tell you. There are two things where in my opinion you were wrong. First, why did you leave the movement?"

"It was after we quarrelled. . . ."

"You can't blame the movement for that."

"I didn't want to see you. I hated you."

"I'm not the only one in the den."

"But you were my best friend. Don't you understand?"

"So why don't you come back now?"

"Because I don't believe in those ideas."

"And did you believe in them then?"

"No. But I believed in you, I admired you and I copied you in everything."

"What have you got against socialism for example?"

"And you, do you believe in socialism? In equality? From each according to his ability and to each according to his needs?"

"Yes, of course, why does it seem so ridiculous to you?"

"Because you've always felt and you still feel that you're superior."

"I don't think I deserve to get more than anybody else."

"And you've got no intention of staying in the movement and going to live on a kibbutz. And you've got every intention of getting into the ROTC, which isn't exactly staying with the youth group in NaHal."

"First, compromise arrangements can be made. Apart from which, there's still a lot of time before the army and a lot of plans can change. And there are still things I can contribute in the movement."

"I haven't got anything to contribute."

"You're cross with me for saying this. But you asked for it."

"On the contrary, I'm grateful to you. What's the second thing?"

"That you should stop worrying and asking whether people like you all the time. It's embarrassing, it's ugly and it's soppy. A person should be able to sense whether he's liked or not and there's no point in talking about it."

This shot went home and hurt Arik to the quick. He knew that Eli was right and he hated himself and his weakness. He felt incapable of continuing the conversation without saying things that he would later regret. So he put on a clownish expression and said in a grotesque, squeaky voice: "Eli, do you like me?"

"Yes, darling," Eli replied in the same comical voice, "I'm crazy about you." And they both burst into laughter intended to put an end to the conversation. A little while later Rachel finished her piano lesson and joined them. Arik accompanied them to the movement den. Naomi was already there, bustling and enthusiastic as usual. As soon as they arrived she came rushing to tell them the news: "You know what, he's got an Arab reed and he plays it wonderfully. I helped him today with literature and suddenly he took his reed out of his satchel, you know the kind, an Arab shepherd's reed. His brother brought it for him from the war, he looted it from some village they conquered. And ever since then he's kept it. I asked him to play me something and he played 'Debka Rafiah,' and he played it really well. He's got a gift for it."

"Why don't you take him to play the accompaniment for your shepherds' dances?" said Arik. "It would be the only authentic thing in the whole performance."

Rachel burst out laughing: "Shut up, Arik, you're not even in the movement, you haven't got the right to criticize."

"Really," said Eli with humourous surprise, "what are you doing here at all? You're not allowed to be in this den that you deserted and betrayed. By the way, why did you leave the movement?"

Naomi sensed that Arik didn't believe that her admiration for Pesach's playing was genuine, that he thought she was convincing herself in order to be kind to Pesach. She was upset. Arik hadn't heard Pesach play, how could he be so sure?

Arik and Naomi had known each other since kindergarten; not like me, who had only joined them in one of the classes of grade school, when I came back to town with my parents. And the relations between them had continued uninterrupted even during the crisis of adolescence with the segregation between the sexes. They were capable of walking side by side in silence without the silence causing them any uneasiness or embarrassment. Even though Arik's cynicism and Naomi's emotionalism made them into two opposites, the secret understanding between them continued; they could almost guess each other's reactions in advance and sensed as if by telepathy what the other was feeling. After walking a ways with Eli and Rachel they parted from them and went home by themselves. Naomi said:

"Lately I've been having the same nightmare almost every night: I wake up in the morning and I can't see anything and I realize that I've gone blind. I want to scream and I can't. Nobody believes me that I'm blind, they're not willing to help me, but I can't see anything and I know that I'll never get better again. And when I wake up, instead of feeling happy and relieved that I'm not blind and it was only a dream, I go on feeling pain and a terrible despair, as if the dream is still going on inside me and the awakening is only a temporary interval."

"Why don't you look it up in Freud's *Interpretation of Dreams*. Maybe you'll find an explanation there," said Arik in a cool, slightly amused tone of voice.

Naomi knew that he didn't like hearing about her dreams, but she went on telling him anyway, because she didn't have anyone else to share them with. And she had to tell somebody. She had never told him about her secret, tortured love for Eli, but she imagined that he must have guessed something. It had gone on for two years already, and begun even before Rachel Hyman's arrival in town. There was no sign that this misery would ever end. There were nights when she tossed and turned, weeping soundlessly and wishing she was dead. Her body was hateful to her, she hated it for having been rejected, for having brought this curse upon her. She knew that she would never be loved and that she was doomed to die an old maid. When she pictured Eli and Rachel's love to herself, she wanted to scream, the pain was so searing. She knew she had no chance of winning his love, that she was banging her head against a stone wall, but there was no power on earth that could drag her away from this wall. A feeling of suffocating humiliation accompanied her wherever she was, whatever she did, in her relations with herself and with others. She could think of nothing else. All the vitality and passion of her youth were invested in the struggle against her misery, and the busy activities with which she tried in vain to distract herself from it.

When she had first fallen in love, about two years before, there was something exhilirating about it. The love filled an empty void in her heart. She felt like the heroine of a novel, she reveled in her secret melancholy and her life took on an hallucinatory quality. Even after she realized that there was no chance of her love being returned, she resolved to live the experience by herself, to taste to the full the beauty and mystery of this most marvelous of human emotions, to keep it all to herself, to cherish it as it was in the first moments of its awakening, to quench her thirst for beauty and purity in it. But she soon realized that she had fallen into a trap and that she was ill with a malignant disease. She became bitter and desperate, the air of the mountain peaks began to suffocate her. And when she lay awake at night she pressed the pillow against her lips so that her parents sleeping in the next room wouldn't hear her sobs. Her whole life was colored by this sickness. Only in the poetry she read and sometimes wrote and kept in a locked drawer, did she find a confidante. Sometimes when she read these poems she heard a friendly voice speaking to her, as if it had been sent especially to comfort her, as if there was somebody in the poetry who remembered her, who thought of her, who understood her suffering. But poetry couldn't save her.

"I'll tell you what your dream means," said Arik.

"Will you?" asked Naomi doubtfully.

"Actually, you want to be blind, in other words, to cling to your inner world and not to see reality."

"Then why does it frighten me and hurt me so much?"

"Because you know it's not true, that you're lying to yourself, that you're not really blind and that you can see reality. You'd like to be blind, to live according to your intentions and not according to the real facts. You know for instance that Pesach's playing on his reed is just nonsense, but you try to persuade yourself and us that he plays wonderfully, that he's got a great gift. Because it suits your intentions, which are probably good, or at any rate, you think they're good."

"How do you know that he doesn't play wonderfully, you've never heard him?"

"It's enough for me that I've heard you. That says everything. But what's worse is the hypocrisy. You all think that you're doing him a favor but you're doing him a great wrong. You're trying to change him, to make him like everybody else. But he's not like everybody else. He's different, and you can't stand for anybody to be different, not to fit in. Everybody has to be the same. You won't let him live the way he wants to live and the way he has to live, according to his nature. You're destroying him little by little, you're castrating him like people castrate a pet cat so it'll get fat and forget everything and only know how to amuse its owners. You're turning him into a hero, you're raising him up only to cast him down in the end and break him. Ever since he grew good-looking you can't stand him keeping to himself and living his own life. The only relations between people that you know are relations of control; ruling or being ruled. You can't come to terms with anyone not taking part in this game, because then he becomes too powerful and he threatens you. That's why society always hates the stranger, the outsider. I don't care about Pesach, I can't stand him and I can't stand types like him, I think he's nothing but an animal, but I care about you, that you're turning into a hypocrite like all the rest of them."

"Why do you say you, you, you? And you, you don't make fun of him all the time, insult him, mock him in your skits?"

"I told you I can't stand him. That's my true feeling about him. I'm not trying to change him, improve him, integrate him into society. That's what you're doing, and that's what I mock and make fun of."

"But he wants it, he wants to be one of us, what right have we to stop him? He's not an animal, he's a human being like anyone else."

"He doesn't really want it. You're playing on his weak spot, which is the same as anybody's weak spot. It's all beginning to flatter him, his head's been turned by the fuss you're all making of him. Nobody could be indifferent to it. That's what I meant when I said that you were castrating him; so that in the end he won't have any powers of resistance and it will be possible to destroy him."

"So in your opinion there's no connection between our true intentions and those we believe are motivating us?"

"In any case, there's no connection between intentions and deeds. Of that I'm sure."

Sometimes Pesach wanted to run far away. He remembered that when he was a child he would run away and once he even hid in a distant citrus grove for a whole day until the workers found him and brought him to the town, where people recognized him and took him home. But when he grew up he dreamed of other places, further away, where he would be able to rest and do as he pleased. When he began to be attracted to girls he pictured this place to himself as the shores of a lake in which naked women bathed at their leisure, like the painting he had seen in the shop that sold pictures next to the big synagogue. He would often study this painting, try to grasp the nature of the women, and choose the most desirable of them. Later, inspired by the movies he saw in the local cinema, he combined the lake with a cowboy ranch. He knew that in order to reach these places he first had to run away. He, who had probably never left the borders of the town and the surrounding citrus groves in his life, planned sensational escapes: to stow away in the hold of a ship sailing to a distant land, to slip across the border into one of the Arab countries, to find a remote, isolated spot in the Negev desert, a place no one knew about, and to build it up by himself. And these plans were always connected with the hiding place where his father hid the money. Accordingly, when Menachem came to ask his father for money one day, he hoped that his father would stand up to him and refuse, even though he loved his brother and it hurt him to see his suffering.

"Where am I supposed to get money from, Menachem?" Pesach's father asked.

"You've got money, I know, you're sitting on it and you don't want to help me," said Pesach's brother, taking a chair from its place by the wall and sitting down next to his father. Pesach himself sat on the couch and listened to their conversation with a poker face.

"I didn't tell you to go and play cards and lose all your money. If you lose you shouldn't play cards," said his father.

"Stop talking shit!" yelled Menachem. "What cards? I'm telling you that I need it to invest in the business. My partner's investing and I have to put something down too, and I haven't got the money. You want me to lose my living? And I've got something coming to me from mother's legacy too."

"Mother's legacy!" Their father burst into bitter laughter. "Perhaps you should go back to the place where you were all those years. They haven't cured you yet."

Menachem's face went white with rage. It was forbidden to mention that place in his hearing.

"You'll pay dearly for this!" he said to his father. "Dearly!" He looked narrowly at Pesach:

"Where did he put the money?"

"I don't know," lied Pesach, who had helped himself to money from the hiding place on more than one occasion.

"Why doesn't he go to work?" shouted Menachem and pointed at his brother. "Why's he wasting our money and his time at high school? He doesn't do anything. What do you want, for him to be a professor?"

"First of all it's not our money, it's my money," their father corrected him calmly, "and secondly I want him to go to school. That's what I want. There'll be plenty of time for him to work later."

The reference to the place where Menachem had spent all those years upset his self-control. He kept looking around as if searching for something to wreak his rage on and break.

"I wouldn't mind going to work," said Pesach, "but he wants me to study."

"Even if I had a lot of money, I wouldn't give you any," said their father provocatively to Menachem. "I've already given you plenty of money and I know what you spent it on: on clothes and girls and cards. That's not what I worked hard all my life for. At your age you can earn your own living. And you know how much it cost us to keep you at that place."

Menachem jumped up as if bitten by a snake and fell upon his father. Pesach rushed up to drag him off, but Menachem fought back and kept screaming: "I'll kill him, I swear I'll kill him!" Pesach overcame him, separated him from his father and held his arms behind his back. Menachem's face was red and his eyes were bloodshot. "Let me go," he said to Pesach, "I won't hurt him." Pesach let go of him and Menachem sat down on his chair. He buried his face in his hands and burst into tears.

"If he thinks his tears will help him he's making a mistake. They don't mean a thing to me," said the father.

Pesach put his hand on his brother's shoulder and tried to calm him. He loved him more than anyone in the world and he couldn't bear to see him like this. Menachem stopped crying and banged his fists on the chair:

"What am I going to I do? What am I going to do?" he mumbled. He turned to Pesach: "I owe money, a lot of money, and I can't pay it back. They won't leave me alone, they'll throw me in jail or else they'll kill me. I'm afraid to show my face in Haifa. They'll find me wherever I am. I'm lost, do you understand?"

Pesach nodded his head understandingly.

"There's no end to it," his father sighed. "The last time I gave him money I told him he wouldn't get any more. Enough! I haven't got it! What am I, a bank? What does he want of my life? Let him get out of the house and out of my sight. I never want to see him again!"

Menachem went to the bathroom, wiped his eyes and combed his hair. For a long time he stood in front of the mirror and examined his face. He put on his coat and when he came back into the room he said to Pesach:

"He'll be sorry for this. Remember what I'm saying to you."

And he walked out of the house and slammed the door.

For a while Pesach dreamed that he would take Nehama the whore with him when he ran away. Nehama wasn't a whore in the true sense of the word, but this was her name in the town. Actually she came from a good family, but when she was a young girl she suddenly went wrong. She kicked over the traces and her lust for men knew no bounds. She began dressing in flashy, vulgar clothes, painted her face with exaggerated makeup and in the evenings she would take the bus to Tel Aviv, sit in bars, and come back late at night drunk, wild, and disheveled, shut herself up in her room in her parents' house and cry. There were people who heard Nehama crying on the summer nights when the windows were open. Her parents bore the disgrace in proud silence and took care of Nehama lovingly and devotedly. She was once a beautiful girl, fair-haired and slender. But the years were unkind to her. She grew fat, her face grew round and double-chinned, her hair, which she started dyeing when it turned darker, lost its vitality, and when she teetered down the street on her stiletto heels there was something coarse, almost bestial, in her appearance. When she met Pesach she was about thirty years old.

It was a few days after his mother died. She was walking down the dirt road that descended from the hill. Pesach stood next to the fence of his house and looked at her. She filled him with desire, not so much because of her external appearance, as because of the promise it suggested, that she might grant him the thing he yearned for so desperately. She was familiar with such looks. She stopped and took off her shoes, as if to shake the dirt out of them. As she did so she leaned against the fence and looked at him appraisingly.

"You live here, Ginger?" she asked him. He nodded and smiled at her. She liked the look of him. She said that she'd lost her way and she didn't know how to get back to the center of town. He realized that she had something else in mind. He led her into the orange grove at the back of the house, and took her right to the end, to a corner where he knew nobody ever went. Nehama fell on him as if she wanted to swallow him alive. When he went back home that evening he knew that he couldn't live without her. After that she came almost every day to the dirt road and he waited for her impatiently and apprehensively: he was afraid that one day she would get sick of him and stop coming. When his status in the class improved and he discovered that there was something about him which set him apart from the other boys and attracted the girls to him, he began to grow a little tired of Nehama. But at the same time he believed that it was she who had brought about the transformation which had turned him into a man, and that if he stopped seeing her the magic might vanish. It never occurred to him that he was a handsome boy. So he went on making love to Nehama in the orange grove and it became a matter of routine. One day she asked him for money. He got up and looked at her body lying at his feet on the ground, with its hunger which could never be satisfied, and he filled with hatred and revulsion for her. He kicked her and said: "Go to hell!" She was stunned by his reaction and called him to come back to her, but he got dressed without even looking at her. "You silly boy, I was only joking!" she called. When he was dressed he kicked her again and said: "Go to hell!" Nehama burst into tears and he left her lying there and went home. Ever since then he hadn't seen or missed her either.

Late at night, when Pesach and his father were sleeping, policemen came and woke them up. Menachem had been caught trying to break into a hardware store. The next morning they went to see him in the police station. Menachem's face was pale and expressionless, his eyes were wide and staring and his hands were blocking his ears as if to protect him from some unbearable noise; as on the day when they had taken him away to that place.

The Sharon Valley was full of mud. Wherever we looked all we saw was mud. Fields, green trees and little houses, and great expanses of dark mud. The water from the rains which had fallen over the past few weeks had not yet seeped into the ground and many pools of water sparkled in the dark mud like windows to the sky. With us in the army truck sat a thin, mustached soldier, wearing a hand-knit skullcap. We didn't know him. He had been sent to be our instructor. He was full of good humor. "Cadets!" he cried loudly, trying to silence the sounds of talking and laughter which filled the truck, "let's try to sing a song, like human beings." And he immediately raised his hand like a conductor and burst into song: "*Said Rabbi Akiva, said Rabbi Akiva, On three things this world stands. . . .*" but we didn't know his songs, silence fell for a moment, and then we burst out laughing. He laughed with us. His name was Yigal, he was a graduate of the Agricultural High School in Pardes Hanna, and he was going to instruct us on planting saplings. Our task was to plant eucalyptus trees in one of the army camps in the Sharon Valley. The whole country was then caught up in a fever of eucalyptus planting. But we had been charged with a special, secret mission: the trees we would plant were intended to camouflage the camp from enemy planes. The work was to last three days and to be conducted in the framework of our national service as cadets. We all took the task seriously and with a feeling of importance except, of course, for Arik, who said provocatively to the instructor:

"But all we'll be doing is giving them a sign—wherever they see eucalyptus trees, they'll know there's an army camp there and bomb it."

"No!" said Yigal. "Little by little the whole country will be covered by eucaplyptuses, like a green curtain, and they won't be able to see a thing."

There was something delightful in this vision of the whole country as a great forest of eucalyptus trees. Eli took his accordion out of its case and played the songs we liked and we sang enthusiastically to assuage our fears of the unknown. We were all wearing old clothes intended to serve as working clothes and boots, and we had brought our good clothes with us in our bags, as instructed. I had never seen my classmates so strangely and wretchedly dressed. In one of the intervals in our singing Arik's voice suddenly became audible, imitating the groaning of a poor, crushed old woman: "Oy, Jews! Where are they taking us? They said it was only to work, but that's what they always say. May God take pity on us!" We all burst out laughing. Only Yigal looked angry and didn't say anything. The truck turned off the highway onto a narrow side road, between citrus groves and avenues of cypresses and acacias. From his place at the back end of the truck Pesach stuck his head out of the opening and his red curls were rumpled by the wind, blown across his forehead and his eyes. The sky was blue and cloudless and the landscape was bathed in the soft light of the beginning of spring. Everything was suffused by the intoxicating smell of orange blossoms.

After a while we arrived at the camp. The truck drove through the gate and stopped and we were told to get off. Not far from the gate a soldier was standing and burning papers in a barrel.

"Jews!" shrieked Arik. "The ghetto's burning!"

Yigal called out: "Line up in rows." We lined up in rows and he stood in front of us with his feet wide apart, his hands behind his hips, erect, his face grim, breathing an air of authority.

"You're in an army camp!" he announced. "And from now on there'll be full military discipline here. You're like soldiers in every respect. What's your name?" He pointed his finger at Arik. Arik mumbled his name. "Step forward and come here." Arik went up to him. "I didn't hear your name." Arik repeated his name aloud. "Your jokes are disgusting, you hear?" yelled Yigal. "I heard what you said in the truck too. You must be sick to make jokes about a subject like that. I could have you court-martialed but this time I'll ignore it. Maybe you didn't know what it means to be in the army yet. How dare you say such things? Is nothing sacred to you? Nobody forced you to come here. If you want to you can leave right now. But if you stay then you'll shut your mouth and behave like everybody else."

Arik was silent. But a faint smile played on his lips and his eyes behind his glasses seemed to say: "See you at the next joke."

We were about thirty boys and girls and we were given one long hut to live in. It was decided that one end would be occupied by the boys, the other end by the girls, and the beds in the middle would remain empty, as a kind of barrier. Naked bulbs dangled in a row from the ceiling of the hut, which was intended to house about fifty soldiers. Each of us grabbed a bed next to his friends and put his things down next to it. I grabbed the bed next to Arik, with Eli in the bed behind him. Arik sat on his bed and looked at his friends busy arranging their belongings, dressed in their strange, shabby outfits and boots. "Look," he said to Eli, "little Polish refugees!"

"Be careful," said Eli, "he's snooping around here and he'll hear you. He's got his eye on you already and if you don't stop making those jokes he can get you into trouble."

"I don't give a damn for him or the rest of the army either," said Arik loudly and defiantly. "Don't be naive. He can't do anything to me. We're not soldiers and he's just trying to scare us."

"That's true," said Eli, "but he can still get you into trouble."

After a while Yigal took us out of the hut in a column of threes and led us to the end of the camp. We stood in an open tin shed in the heart of a big stretch of ground surrounded by barbed wire on three sides. In the shed were hundreds of rusty tins containing eucalyptus saplings and a big pile of spades and hoes. There was a pleasant warmth in the air. The camp itself was ugly and quite dilapidated: a collection of big, old wooden huts in the heart of a flat expanse of dense, dark mud. The smell of the blossoms reached us, but the fields and the groves were out of sight, except for a strip of green, far beyond the boundaries of the camp, on the horizon. We stood next to the thin ropes stretched out to mark the rows of trees, the boys digging the pits and the girls putting in the saplings and patting down the soil around them. Our boots were soon covered with mud and it didn't take long before the rest of us was too, to everyone's delight.

At midday we were led into the mess, where the soldiers were busy eating their lunch. We looked at them with a certain revulsion. They were different from the soldiers we had known up to now, or imagined in our hearts. Most of them were new immigrants, short and glum-faced, ill at ease in the uniforms which didn't fit them, mumbling in broken Hebrew or foreign languages. There was something depressing about the sight of these soldiers, we had never seen people like them before. They looked more like prisoners-of-war or convicts serving life sentences than warriors. Apart from them, there were a handful of real soldiers in the mess, men and women, who had an idle and carefree air.

In the afternoon there was a competition. Yigal announced that the couple who planted the greatest number of trees in the allotted time would get a badge. He even showed us the badge which was made of bronze and had a spade decorated with a branch (of a eucalyptus, no doubt) painted on it. All the boys found girl partners and the sign to begin was given. After a while Pesach and his partner could be seen passing everybody else as they advanced rapidly up their row. Pesach sprang from pit to pit digging with diabolical speed and when he saw that his partner couldn't keep up with him he stopped digging and went back to help her plant. After which he bounded back to the place he had reached before and resumed his digging. It was a riveting spectacle. As soon as he finished digging one pit he glided on to the next one, the movements of the spade in his hands and all the movements of his body were supple, precise, round, soft and astonishingly beautiful, like movements in a dance. We all stopped working to watch him. Even Yigal the instructor was wide-eyed in astonishment, and said that even in the Agricultural School of Pardes Hanna he had never seen anything like it. When Pesach and his partner finished their row they stood at the end of it and looked back at us. The girl was panting for breath, but Pesach broke into triumphant laughter. We had never seen him laugh like this before, full-throatedly, wholeheartedly, slapping his thighs in enjoyment. Accustomed mainly to his smiles and his silences, we now heard his peals of laughter come rolling down the field toward us.

The prize-giving was only to take place after we had all finished planting our rows. In the meantime Pesach and his partner waited next to the instructor. When we reached them, everyone surrounded Pesach, praising him to the skies and slapping him on the back and shoulders, and he laughed again. Something opened up in him at those moments, he beamed with happiness and strength and pride. For the first time it was evident that he really felt like one of us. Yigal insisted on holding a ceremony. We were ordered to form up in threes, opposite the winners of the competition. When Yigal went up to pin the badge on the winner's collar, Pesach burst out laughing again, as if it was all a joke and he refused to take it seriously.

In the evening we returned to the hut and sat down on our beds. Arik lay flat on his back and seemed to be feeling unwell. A few of the girls began singing Russian songs in two parts and Eli joined in and accompanied them on his accordion. Little by little everybody gathered in the girls' section and joined in the singing. Pesach lay across one of the girls' beds, his head resting on her thigh, his feet touching the floor and tapping in time to the music. I asked Arik what the matter was. He took off his glasses and put them on the windowsill at his head. He rubbed his eyes. They were red, as if he had been crying. He complained of a headache. At this time of the year everything was in bloom and the blossoming made his eyes burn. This sounded strange to me but I imagined it was connected with his illness. When I tried to inquire further into the effect of the blossoming on his illness he avoided answering me.

In the girls' section the enthusiasm increased. They pushed the beds together until they made one enormous bed and they all sprawled out on it in a heap, boys and girls together, the boys leaning on the girls and hugging their shoulders, and Eli sitting in the middle and playing the Russian evening songs, full of sweet melancholy, on his accordion. Rachel Hyman, her head on his knees, conducting the singing with her hand.

I tried to cheer Arik up. "You remember, once you told me that society should give young people a framework for free sexual activity? Here you are—" I pointed to the group on the pushed-together beds, "your demands have been met."

Arik smiled wearily, without even turning his head in the direction I was pointing in. "You know," he said, "in primitive societies they hold initiation rites for adolescents, they isolate them from the tribe, collect them in a special place and the elders explain what's permitted and what's forbidden, how to act with a woman, everything by means of ceremonies and religious rituals. That's how they become men. When they leave that place they're free to make love to any available girl. Nice, no? But with us it's eucalyptuses and youth movement songs."

I joined the singers. I was drawn to the unity of the group. Naomi sang with her eyes closed and a lot of feeling, as usual. When she noticed me next to her, she whispered in my ear in order not to disturb the singing: "Look how beautiful she is." And she jerked her chin in the direction of Rachel Hyman, who was sitting in the middle of the group, her head on Eli's leg and her long, smooth hair loose on her shoulders, her neck long and white and slender, and the big khaki shirt she had apparently borrowed from her older brother lying on her body with a sloppiness that was full of grace. Her feet, clad in thin white socks, were tucked under her knees. Her big, black, slightly slanting eyes were pensive and dreamy. Eli sitting behind her smiled his calm, generous, heart-warming smile. One of the girls suddenly cried out in coy complaint: "Pesach's putting his hands where they don't belong!" Pesach laughed: "Oh no I'm not, maybe you'd like me to, but I won't do you that favor." The girl's friend said: "Don't tell such fibs, I saw you too!" And the two girls burst out laughing and began to confer in whispers. Pesach said: "I don't know where my hands are, if anyone comes close to them—it's her own lookout." None of the girls sitting next to him moved away.

Yigal came into the hut and was evidently pleased by the sociable atmosphere. "Lights out, boys and girls!" he called. The group broke up and moved the beds back into their places. Yigal had brought a length of thin rope with him, the same rope as that used to mark the rows of trees for planting, and stretched it across the room, tying the ends to the handle of a window on either side. Then he hung a few blankets on the rope, making a curtain to hide the girls' beds from our eyes. He stepped back to examine his handiwork. He was satisfied. At the same time he noticed Arik lying on his bed, isolated from the group in the girls' sector. He went up to him.

"What's the matter with you? Why aren't you with everybody else?"

"I don't feel like it," said Arik wearily.

"I suppose you came here to lower everybody's morale?"

Arik didn't reply. Eli, who saw the two of them talking from a distance, was afraid of trouble and came running up to Arik's bed.

"What's up?" he asked. "Has he said something already?"

Yigal laughed: "Why do you come running to his rescue all the time? What are you, his keeper?"

The instructor waited for everyone to get into bed, wished us goodnight, switched off the lights and left the hut. The minute we heard the door closing everyone began laughing and talking, as if the fact that we were actually going to sleep there was too much for us to take in, and the whole thing was only some kind of a game. Suddenly the door opened, the lights went on and Yigal stood on the threshold frowning angrily. "Lights out," he called, "that means absolute silence. Anyone who says a word after I switch off the light will be expelled from the hut and go to sleep with the RPs!" He stood there in the light for a minute in silence, to emphasize his words, and then switched off the light. Then he waited in the dark for a minute longer, and went out closing the door behind him. The threat worked. None of us wanted to sleep apart from the group, and I supposed that they all, like me, imagined the mysterious RPs, in whose company it was apparently a dreadful punishment to sleep, in the shape of the new immigrants we had seen sitting in the mess or huddling between the huts in the camp, gloomy and foreign and persecuted-looking.

There was a silence in the hut, broken only by the sound of breathing and an occasional cough or creaking bed. Sadness gripped me and I couldn't fall asleep. The army issue woolen blankets were prickly and strange and they had a bad smell, the smell of the soldiers who had used them before me, which stuck to them and which I couldn't stand. The bed was uncomfortable. Outside I could hear the frogs croaking. There was always a chorus of frogs sawing away in the background of my first night away from home and it was always a sad night, full of regrets. I had come to realize that in my life things happened to me twice, repeating themselves as if time had held up a mirror to them. Of all the trips I had been on I now remembered the class hike in the last grade of primary school. We had gone to the Galilee and slept outside in a wood on the banks of the lake. And there too the loathsome croaking of the frogs had rasped in the silence, and like then now too I couldn't sleep and my heart was bitter. All the events of the day and the prospect of the days and nights to come seemed to me dull, futile and oppressive. I heard sounds of rhythmic breathing around me and I knew that everybody was falling asleep. The pale light from the lamps outside the windows cast spots on some of the beds and the floor of the hut. The sounds of laughter and nailed boots on the concrete and talking in Arabic rose outside and receded until they were heard no more. And again the chorus of frogs ruled the roost, rasping and creaking with tireless, diabolical persistence. I longed for my room and my parents and my little brother all fast asleep at home.

Suddenly I heard a movement to my right. I looked in that direction and behind Arik's bed I saw Eli slowly removing his blankets, sitting up in bed and looking around him. Then he rose slowly to his feet, trying not to make a noise, and stood there in his underpants. He scanned the beds on both sides of the hut to make sure that everyone was sleeping. I closed my eyes and pretended to be asleep. But I immediately opened them again and saw his silhouette slipping behind the blankets curtaining off the girls' quarters. A moment later I saw him coming back with Rachel, the two patches of her bra and panties pale on her dark silhouette. They were carrying Rachel's clothes, blankets and sheets in their arms, and they proceeded to lay their burden down on one of the empty beds in the no-man's-land on this side of the curtain. Silently they made the bed and then they got into it and pulled the blankets up over their heads. I watched the scene out of the corner of my eye. It was steeped in a dream-like light. The two silhouettes silently and swiftly making their bed looked to me like gods. I didn't hear a sound nor could I see any movement whatsoever in the blankets covering them because of the distance of their bed from mine. But I sensed their presence vividly, filling my heart and the whole dark hut with a mist of beauty and mystery and with longings not to be borne. The door in the girls' quarters opened. Someone went outside.

I turned onto my other side, toward Arik's bed. There were about two meters separating our beds. The window at our heads shed a pale light onto his bed and above the mound of blankets I could see the phosphorescent numbers on the face of his watch and his two eyes glittering in the dark. I wanted to say something to him, to share my feelings with him, but I was too far away from him to whisper softly enough for only him to hear.

Naomi saw him going up to Rachel's bed in his underpants. Rachel was waiting for him. As soon as he passed the screen, she sat up in bed. Naomi's heart pounded violently. She felt as if her bed were moving in time to the pounding. Please God, no! she begged silently, only not that, here, now, in front of me. Rachel rose quickly from her bed and gathered up her sheets and blankets, deposited part of the bundle in Eli's arms, picked up her clothes, and the two of them slipped past the screen. Naomi didn't know where they were going, but their silhouette remained in front of her, vivid and burning, in the place where they had been standing a moment before, refusing to disappear, as if it had been branded on the retina of her eye forever. She saw him embracing her and kissing her on the mouth. For a long time they went on embracing in front of her and she closed her eyes in unendurable pain. And still they stood before her embracing, silent, thirsty for the touch of love.

She felt hot in bed in spite of the shivering which had taken hold of her. She threw off one of the two blankets and turned over. Her head felt very heavy. A feeling of suffocation clutched at her throat. She tried to distract herself from the pain, repeating to herself like an invocation verses of poems that she had loved, in which she had heard an inner voice speaking to her—perhaps they would have it in their power to transport her magically to another place, to repose, to purity. *Today my soul desires / to dwell in You, forgotten. / You are a dense forest to me, / oppressive and sad. / If only You could see / how between night and dawn, / my hands plead at your door— / to let me return!* But her body rebelled and would not obey her. She felt very nauseous and sensed that she would have to go outside to vomit. Naomi got out of bed, wrapped herself in a blanket and went quietly out the door in the corner of the girls' quarters. Outside the sky was cold and clear. She shuffled over to the toilet and vomited there. When she recovered from vomiting she went over to the tap next to the concrete platform outside the hut and washed her face. She felt a little better and she sat down on the edge of the concrete and looked at her watch. She looked up at the sky, and breathed in deep lungfuls of the night air to strengthen herself. For a long time she sat outside looking at the sky. Again and again she tried to exert herself and find something to do, to occupy herself with some calming thought, to sink into a liberating fantasy, but she found nothing. She tried to stand up but heavy weights pinned her legs down. She didn't know where to go or why, but she felt that sitting there at that moment was too much for her to bear. Underneath the army blanket enveloping her, her body was still being shaken by the wild, rebellious beating of her heart, as if it were trying to break its bonds. She was afraid that this time she would not be strong enough to resist. She covered her head with the blanket and tried to cry. But the pain stuck deep in her throat and chest and refused to dissolve. Nevertheless she remained with her head wrapped in the blanket. The pair of embracing shadows appeared again and again and she could not send them away. Perhaps she could stay there forever, she said to herself, underneath the blanket, as if inside a closed tent, sealed up, without air, without seeing anything, without hearing anything, without anybody seeing her, and little by little come to an end, disappear, because it was impossible to continue in this place and there was no other place where she could go and it was impossible even to get up or change her position and it was impossible too, to sweeten the pain with hope that a change would actually change anything; all possibilities were closed underneath this blanket and the world outside was sinking and disappearing and all that remained were two shadows embracing in the dark, alone, at the end of the road, at the end of all the roads.

She tried to spread out her hands in order to open the edges of the blanket wrapped round her head but her arms refused to obey her, her elbows were pinned to her chest as if they had frozen with the rest of her body and she couldn't bring her arms back to life and make them move. The air inside the blanket was hot and stifling and she couldn't breathe. Maybe this is it, maybe it's come, maybe it's beginning to happen, like this, without an inkling in advance, in a slow sinking. A passing hope of release and rest brought with it the actual flavor of release and rest, but this imaginary relief only lasted for a moment for from somewhere deep inside her an impulse of fear suddenly stirred. Her body panicked and protested, due to the lack of air or perhaps to the dangerous thought, a shudder ran through her and her hands suddenly opened the edges of the blanket and exposed her face. The cool night air was sharp, bracing, and full of the smell of orange blossoms. For a moment she felt a kind of intoxication and she lost her sense of balance and her body swayed. She opened her eyes and breathed in the air, as she had done when she first sat down on the concrete platform after she vomited. The frisson of fear and danger which had alerted her in spite of herself aroused dormant sources of strength and the will to overcome. Gradually her heart stopped pounding. She went on sitting there for a while and weariness descended on her. She looked at her watch and saw that only twenty minutes had passed since she had left the hut. Judging by her weariness she had imagined that many hours had passed outside and that it would soon be dawn. When she felt that she would be able to sleep she stood up and entered the hut. She stood still for a moment until her eyes grew accustomed to the dark, and examined the beds of her friends who were sleeping a deep, sweet, peaceful sleep. Rachel's bed was still empty. Naomi slipped the blanket off her body and spread it on her other blankets, climbed under them and closed her eyes. At long last the pair of embracing silhouettes had ceased to haunt her and a moment of calm was about to descend. Naomi knew these false calms that sometimes descended on her at moments of busy activity or in the great weariness after the struggles, after the despair. She knew that these lulls would not last more than a moment, like the mirages that appeared to people lost in the desert, but she abandoned herself to them with all the powers of oblivion that she could find within her.

I woke up with the first light. Everyone was sleeping around me. I looked immediately at Rachel and Eli's bed. It was empty and tidy as it had been in the evening and Eli was sleeping in the bed behind Arik's. I began to doubt whether I had seen what I had seen in the night or if it had been a dream. Arik was snoring faintly in his sleep. His hand dangled from the bed, limp as the hand of the dead. But the watch on his wrist reminded me of the night and of his eyes which I had seen awake in the darkness. He had been a witness to what had happened. My heart was still sore from the evening before, and the two days and two nights remaining seemed very long and wearisome. In the row opposite me I saw Pesach's bed. He was covered to the waist and his mouth was open in his sleep. He was sleeping in his muddy work clothes and the prize badge was pinned to his collar. In the girls' quarters a stir began. Someone apparently woke up and went out of the hut. I did not feel the warmth toward those sleeping around me that I had felt the night before when we sang together. They were so alien to me and their company was enforced and oppressive.

After a long time Yigal came into the hut to wake us up with a shout of "Good morning!" The faces of the sleepers emerged from the blankets, creased in expressions of pain and exhaustion, as if they had returned from an agonizing and backbreaking journey. The sounds of chattering and laughter were no longer heard. Eli got up first, his face serious, almost grim. He took his toilet bag and towel and went outside. Arik fell asleep again. I woke him up and he said: "Yes, the little Polish refugees have to get up now," and smiled a myopic and despairing smile. When we lined up for the morning parade I saw that everyone looked glum. I imagined that they were all feeling like me. I soon discovered that Eli and Rachel were not together. When we sat down to breakfast in the mess too, they sat apart, she with her girlfriends, and he with us. I wondered what had happened between them in the night. Every now and then Eli stole a quick look at her and then withdrew into himself again. Arik, who was apparently familiar with these moods and who perhaps knew what had happened between them in the night, refrained from talking to him.

We went out to the planting area and worked unenthusiastically. Toward noon two girl soldiers came to watch Pesach at work. They were apparently friends of Yigal's and he must have told them about the competition. They wanted to see if he hadn't exaggerated in his description. But Pesach too worked without zest. They went up to him and he turned his head curiously in their direction. In the looks of one of them, a plump blonde with a pretty face, he read the call familiar to him. He smiled his mysterious smile at her, and narrowed his eyes with his hands on his hips. She said to him with an arch smile: "Go on, Ginger, do it like you did it yesterday in the competition." He said: "I don't want to, there's no competition now," and laughed.

At lunch Pesach sat with her at the soldiers' table and showed no signs of feeling ill at ease among them. His mood had grown slightly more cheerful since morning, but the same could not be said of Eli, who hardly spoke to anyone and was unable to disguise his unhappiness. Naomi looked at him appraisingly from time to time, and he sensed her looks and once he even glared at her. Rachel, who was sitting with her friends, succeeded better than Eli in hiding her mood, but every now and then it showed. I looked from one to the other, and even this estrangement between them seemed to me to be wrapped in a dreamy beauty, as if the vestiges of the magic of the night were still clinging to it, as if it added another dimension of mystery to the pair of naked silhouettes who had prepared the bed for them to lie on and who even now followed Rachel and Eli everywhere, like faithful guards. I didn't speak to Arik about what had happened between Eli and Rachel in the night, not only because I was afraid he would sneer at me for my curiosity, but also because the scene was very dear to my heart, and I wanted to keep it still shrouded in secrecy, the way it was.

On our return to the hut in the evening the beds in the girls' quarters were pushed together again, but our hearts weren't into singing. Instead we talked, and Arik, whose good mood had come back to him during the day, was in brilliant form and made us all laugh and teased the girls about their insatiable lust for the charms of the beautiful Pesach. We urged him to write the skits and the humorous songs for the party on the last night. He said that he would write them only if he was excused from planting the next day. Naomi, who was responsible for the party, promised to persuade Yigal to agree to this concession. Once again warmth and friendship reigned, but Eli and Rachel still hadn't exchanged a word and sat far apart from each other. Pesach stood up suddenly and left the group. He went to his bed and picked up his grey battledress jacket. We guessed that he had a date with the blonde soldier and we smiled at him. A few of us made joking remarks. But he didn't smile back at us, or laugh as he had been doing lately, and instead he threw the battledress angrily onto his bed and looked at us sullenly and suspiciously. That look of the wild animal warning you not to come near gleamed in his eyes again. He was no longer one of us, but a hostile stranger alert for danger. He looked us over one by one, bent over his bed again, took the battledress and walked out of the hut.

We looked at each other in astonishment. "What's the matter with him?" asked Naomi. "Did you see the hatred he looked at us with?" She sounded personally insulted.

"He really does hate us," said Arik. "And he's right. We're driving him crazy."

"What harm have we done him, for instance?" asked Eli with ostentatious irony.

"In the space of a few months we changed our attitude to him and transformed him from a nonentity into a hero. You think it's possible to adjust to that?"

"But he changed!" cried Rachel Hyman. "And we're the ones who haven't yet adjusted to it."

"We've all changed," pronounced Eli thoughtfully, "everything's changed." And it was impossible to tell from his voice whether he was stating this fact with satisfaction or resentment. But for some reason it seemed to me that he was saying it mainly about himself and what was happening to him. As he spoke, Rachel looked at him from where she was sitting, the expression on her face saying plainer than words: Indeed? And Arik lowered his eyes as if he were ashamed to meet Eli's eyes. I had the feeling that Arik too knew what had happened between Eli and Rachel and that the three of them shared a scret which I didn't know. And suddenly this hurt me very much and I was no longer satisfied with the beauty of the mystery. I had the impression that they were talking about Pesach and referring to something else, that they were talking a symbolic language, a kind of code which enabled them to bare their souls to each other without anyone else understanding. And I had not been found worthy to be included in their secret.

"He's got the strength of a man and the sense of a baby," said one of the girls and burst into loud laughter at the sound of her own words.

"That's not true," protested Naomi. "You don't know him. He's got as much sense as any of us."

"Sometimes he looks at us," said one of the boys, "with a kind of contempt, as if he feels sorry for us, as if we're ignorant babies compared to him."

"Growing up," said Eli, "is waking from a dream. I'm not saying it's a good dream or a bad dream—but it's necessary to wake up from it."

"To wake up from a dream," said Arik, "is also to betray it."

Eli frowned, as if he couldn't understand what he was getting at. He looked at Arik with a kind of resentment:

"What obligations has a person got toward his dreams?"

"Dreams are the truest and deepest thing about a person," said Naomi.

"But they've got nothing to do with practical behavior in daily life. On the contrary," argued Eli, "all they can do is interfere with right thinking and logic."

"But life isn't just logic and right thinking!" cried Naomi passionately. "Our feelings influence us no less than our reason, perhaps more: there's a constant struggle between them."

"More's the pity," said Eli. "I don't envy anyone in that position."

"Some people haven't got any feelings," said Rachel. "Like people who are color-blind. It's like a birth defect." She left no doubt as to whom she had in mind.

Arik rose: "I have the feeling now that I have to go and crap."

"Don't betray that dream," laughed Eli; for the first time that day we saw him laugh.

Arik went out into the dark. The cold had chased the few soldiers on the base into the barracks whose little lights were scattered about the empty wastes of grey mud. He walked a bit and saw the little silhouettes of two guards patrolling the fence, their guns on their shoulders, conversing with broad gestures. Because of the distance he could barely hear their voices. They went on pacing and disappeared behind a building which hid the fence. Arik suddenly smiled to himself: If I went and pulled up all the eucalyptuses we planted. . . . Tomorrow morning they'd see them . . . hundreds and hundreds of uprooted little eucalyptuses, lying on the ground with their roots in the air! He couldn't control his laughter as he imagined the instructor Yigal discovering this sight. He went on walking along the path trodden in the mud. He hated the group heart-to-hearts which had become so frequent during the past year and which invariably concluded with an argument about the existence of God. He regretted remaining in the hut and not leaving before and saying what he had said about betraying dreams. His feet led him, perhaps out of the habit of the past two days, to the planting area. As he approached the open shed holding the saplings, he saw a figure sitting with its back to one of the wooden poles supporting the roof. When he came closer he saw that it was Pesach. For a moment he was alarmed and afraid that the blonde soldier was there too hiding somewhere in the dark, and that he was intruding on their privacy. But Pesach was sitting alone and when he saw Arik he shouted angrily: "What do you want?"

"Nothing," said Arik, "I was just going for a walk. I didn't know you were there."

"So now you know," said Pesach.

Arik turned on his heel and began to retrace his steps.

"Come here a minute," called Pesach.

Arik returned.

"I wanted to hit you plenty of times but I know you're weak and I controlled myself."

"Why did you want to hit me?"

"Because you get on my nerves with your wisecracks."

Arik was silent. He looked at Pesach sitting in front of him with his elbows on his knees and saw his cat's eyes glittering at him in the darkness.

"I hate you," said Pesach.

Arik wondered why these words hurt him so much. Did words have the power to hurt as such, regardless of who said them? Or perhaps the thirst for affection and appreciation was so strong that even this creature's affection was now necessary to him? And perhaps, all unconsciously, what had happened to everyone else had happened to him too, and Pesach now played a part in his psyche, had become one of his heroes too?

"Because I'm weak?"

"No. Because you insult people all the time. You've got no shame. You think you're cleverer than everybody else. You think I don't know they're making fun of me? I know everybody's making fun of me and I don't give a damn. They make fun of you too, behind your back, what do you think?"

"But that's not true," said Arik, "nobody makes fun of you, you simply don't understand what's going on."

"Don't worry," said Pesach, "I understand what's going on very well. But I don't care. Next week I'm quitting school anyway and

going to work till I'm drafted. You won't see 'beautiful Pesach' any
more."

"You were insulted because I said you were beautiful?" said Arik
in a puzzled tone.

"People don't say things like that. I'm not a girl."

"Is that why you walked out of the hut?"

"I can't stand it any longer."

"Everyone thought you had a date with the blonde."

"It's none of anybody's business where I go."

"Listen," said Arik in sudden excitement, "beauty is the most
wonderful thing in the world. It's the only thing worth living for. I
wish I was beautiful—I'd give anything. . . ."

"You really are ugly," Pesach interrupted him, "you look like
an old woman."

"I know," said Arik.

"You can go back to your mates in the hut now and make fun
of what I said to you."

"I won't even talk about it," said Arik. "Believe me, I won't
make fun of you, I promise; do you believe me?"

"I told you, I don't care."

"But I care if you believe me; I promise you."

"Okay, okay, now go away," said Pesach impatiently.

Arik turned round and walked away. He didn't understand
what had happened to him, why he had been so excited and why
he had said the things he said. Again he felt a miserable sense of
failure and the feeling that that there was no connection between
what he did and what happened to him. He stood still and looked
back. Pesach had disappeared. The shed was empty. Perhaps he
had a date with the blonde soldier after all?

By the time Arik returned to the hut everyone had already made
their beds even though Yigal hadn't yet come to announce lights
out. Eli was already in bed. We were all still tired from the night
before. Arik sat down on the edge of Eli's bed.

"It took you a long time," smiled Eli.

"I wandered round the base a bit," said Arik. "I had a fantastic
idea: imagine if I went out now and pulled up all the saplings

we planted over the past two days. Tomorrow morning when we went out to work, he'd see it. Imagine the look on his face! Even in Pardes Hanna they never saw the like!"

They both burst out laughing and Eli said: "My but you're a negative, destructive type—an enemy of the people, that's what you are!"

When Yigal came in to switch off the lights, he noticed Pesach's empty bed and asked where Ginger was. Eli jumped up immediately and said that he had gone to the toilet.

"Good night," said Yigal. He switched off the light and left.

There was no more talking or laughter. Weariness defeated us. I welcomed it. I knew that tonight I would find solace in it for the painful alienation and regrets I had suffered the night before. There were already sounds of rhythmic breathing and I heard Arik's faint snoring and wondered if this time Eli was going to sleep in his own bed all night. But I knew that even if another visionary scene took place in the night, I wouldn't see it. The blankets were no longer so prickly or disgusting in the smell of others clinging to them and the bed was no longer so uncomfortable and the pleasant heaviness spread through me and when I was on the verge of falling asleep, I heard the door of the hut open. I opened my eyes and saw Pesach groping his way slowly between the beds until he reached his own. He took off his battledress, kicked off his shoes, and got under the blankets with his clothes on.

When we went out to the planting area in the morning Arik remained in the hut with Naomi and a couple of other girls who had been let off work to make preparations for the party in the evening. He had been given permission to remain in the hut and write his skits. "In any case he doesn't do anything except make fun of the work, disturb the others and lower the morale," said Yigal, "so he might as well be of some use." Yigal attributed great importance to the group "folklore" and the party which was to be its pinnacle. The girls busied themselves with decorating the hut and preparing the refreshments, and Naomi directed the work efficiently and with

her usual enthusiasm. And while her friends glued paper chains together, she approached Arik who had retired to a corner of the hut
to compose his skits. On a sheet of paper she had written, next to
the many organizational details she had to remember, the artistic
program: community singing accompanied by Eli, a performance
by Pesach on his Arab shepherd's reed, a poem of Alterman's read
by her, Arik's skits, refreshments and dancing. When Arik's eyes
fell on Pesach's performance, he pulled a face:

"Are you nuts? What's that good for?"

"Arik, I don't want to discuss it any more. You've never heard
him play and you just hate him. It's wonderful, believe me."

"Naomileh," said Arik, "I'm sure that you mean well. So listen
to me, leave it alone. You're not doing him a favor. Does Eli know
about it?"

"Of course," said Naomi, "he's going to accompany him on the
accordion. He's thinks it's a nice idea too."

"Ah," said Arik, "they're going to play together. Good. That's
okay then."

At the planting the mood was elated. In anticipation of our departure Eli relaxed the reins of discipline and the pace of the work.
He made jokes all the time. Eli and Rachel were together again,
and just as I didn't know what had happened between them that
night, I didn't know what had led to their reconciliation either. In
the jollity which had descended on everyone and infected me as
well, many things in my memory of the past two days became
blurred, everything was effaced by the agreeable feeling that we
were happy here, that it was wonderful to be together and a shame
that it was all about to end. Pesach was in high spirits, and his
sullen exit from the hut the evening before was forgotten too.
After all, we knew that he had found consolation in the arms of
the blonde soldier, who for some reason had not appeared in the
mess that morning. After a while there were no more saplings left
in the shed and no work left for us to do. We all sat down and
sang. Yigal insisted on teaching us songs from the religious youth
movement, some of which were really nice.

"This evening at the party," said Yigal, "I want it to be really jolly. I want the whole camp to hear. There won't be any lights-out and as far as I'm concerned you can go on dancing and having fun till morning."

"Wait until you hear Arik's skits and imitations," said Rachel. "His imitations are so funny you can die laughing."

"And you, Ginger, who will you imitate at the party?" asked Yigal, who had a soft spot for Pesach ever since he had won the competition. Pesach, who remembered that he was supposed to keep his performance a secret, said: "I'll imitate a hyena. Have you ever heard a hyena laughing at night?"

He stood up, cupped his hands round his mouth, raised his face to the sky and broke into a long howl which turned into a kind of cruel laughter full of suffering and malicious glee at once. A high, plaintive scream, rising and falling, growing closer and louder and receding into the distance. We saw the veins on his neck swelling with the effort and this howl of laughter had no end, Pesach's breath was so long. When he finished his face was red and he took deep breaths of air. He looked pleased with his success, for everyone cheered him and Yigal said:

"That's exactly what it sounds like! There were nights when we had a hyena prowling round in our fields. Sometimes it sounded as if it was next to the house, right opposite the window. It was scary. When we heard that terrible laugh, it froze our blood. We never saw it. For us it was only a voice, but like the voice of a human being laughing in hatred and a terrible cruel pain. It sounded just like that, just like he imitated it. And because of that laughter a lot of legends have grown up around the hyena. They say that first he cruelly devours the carcasses of his victims, and then he laughs at them with hatred and mockery. Of course that's all nonsense. In the end we once saw a dead hyena. And what did we see? A wretched animal that scavenges carcasses for food and that's more frightened of us than we are of it. And the laughter of the hyena isn't laughter at all. Animals don't know how to laugh. It's a signal to the other members of the pack and a love call to the female in the mating season. It's their language, like the dog's bark and the jackal's howl and so on."

From here Yigal proceeded to his favorite subject: the folklore of the Pardes Hanna Agricultural School. And we listened gladly to his stories because we were in a good mood and we liked the soldier in the hand-knit skullcap and were sorry that we were soon to part and would never meet again. Thus the day passed until evening was about to fall. Before we dispersed Yigal reminded us to wash ourselves and put on the good clothes we had been told to bring with us. "Anyone in work clothes will be thrown out of the party. And make sure it's a good party because I'm bringing guests with me."

Judging by the amused and mysterious expression on his face we guessed that he meant the two girl soldiers, one of whom was Pesach's lover.

I imagined that for most of us this was the first time we had showered in public. I wondered if everyone felt as ashamed as I did at being seen naked and even more at seeing the nakedness of their friends. But I knew that it would be more shameful to shirk this necessity, in other words to confess to the shame, to give it so explicit a name. Accordingly, we set off in a noisy procession for the showers, towels on our shoulders, and Arik, who was marching in front of me, turned round and smiled with the bleak smile of a man being led to the gallows. I remembered what he had told me of the coming-of-age rites in primitive tribes. Maybe this too was a kind of rite which had to be undergone one day. There was something suspect in the artificial hilarity and animation which accompanied our procession to the showers; it was obvious that we were encouraging ourselves, calming our fears and appeasing the evil spirits like tribal warriors going to battle. Only Pesach was not among us. Was he so ashamed of his nakedness, or was it another one of his mysterious disappearing acts? It was clear to me that everybody felt as I did, but the common distress did nothing to strengthen my spirit, and only confirmed my fears.

There was a bad smell in the soldiers' showerhouse, which seemed to me only too suitable as a background to the scene about to take place in it.

"Hey, there's no light!" shouted someone. "The globe must be broken."

A couple of experts went up to the switch and fiddled around with it, but to no avail. They looked for another switch and didn't find one. I saw relief spread over my friends' faces. It was dusk and the showers were already in semi-darkness.

"All we need now is for there to be no hot water," said Eli. He was the first to undress and he turned on the water in the shower. It was evident that he was truly unashamed of his nakedness. The water was hot and plentiful. Gradually we all got undressed and tried to act very naturally, but even in the dim light it was possible to sense the averted faces and the fear, the embarrassment, and the haste to get it over with and forget about it as quickly as possible. But after the first, miserable moment, there was a sudden surge of joy. It passed between us like some liberating electricity and I felt it together with everyone else. Something happened to us and we didn't know what it was. We looked directly at each other's bodies without any sense of guilt. As if the disgrace of the body had been lifted from us forever, as if it had been washed away in the shower, together with the sweat and the dust which had stuck to us over the past three days, and we would never know its humiliating taste again. The sense that we had undergone a difficult test together and the knowledge that it was only by being together that we had prevailed, filled our hearts with feelings of mutual gratitude and fraternity and the only way to express the joy of this liberation was without words and sentences, but in loud shouts and unintelligible howls.

When we emerged clean and pure from the ritual bathing, it was already completely dark outside and a mighty song burst out of us, the paean of victory of those returning from the final battle.

The whole appearance of the hut had altered. Paper chains festooned it from wall to wall and the naked bulbs had been covered with colored cardboard shades. All the boys' beds had been joined together and arranged in a semicircle to serve as seats. The area vacated was intended for dancing. Blankets had been hung on the rope separating the girls quarters from us again, to enable them to get dressed when they came back from the girls' showers. We too got dressed. After we had grown accustomed to seeing each other in old, mud-stained work clothes for the past three days, our white shirts shone with an exaggerated kind of festivity. Our wet hair gleamed in the lights of the hut. Pesach came in, his towel over his shoulders and his hair wet. After he had preceded us to the showers and discovered that the lights weren't working, one of the soldiers had directed him elsewhere, to a newer, nicer shower.

Naomi emerged from the girls' quarters in an embroidered blouse and a dark blue pleated skirt. Under her arm was the book of poems. She called to behind the screen: "Is everyone ready?" and when the answer came in the affirmative, she pulled the blankets off the rope and one of the girls came to fold them. Next to the wall stood long trestle tables, covered with sandwiches, soft drinks and sweets. A wave of pride and affection welled up in us for our girls, who had taken the trouble to prepare all this, and done it so well.

"Don't anyone dare touch the refreshments!" Naomi announced.

"Don't worry," called Eli, "I'll stand guard."

Naomi left the hut and went to stand under the lamp, to be alone with the Alterman poem she was going to read at the party. She had been so busy organizing that she hadn't had time to prepare for her reading with the seriousness and thoroughness she devoted to everything she did. She was concentrating on the page in front of her when suddenly she saw Pesach emerging from the hut and coming toward her.

"I have to roll up my sleeves," said Pesach, "and I don't know how to do it. It doesn't come out right. Could you roll them up for me?"

Naomi laid the book down at her feet on the concrete platform and when she straightened up Pesach raised his hand and put it on her shoulder. She began to roll his sleeve up. She saw the planter's badge glittering on the collar of the white shirt and suddenly she felt the tips of his fingers touching her neck. A shudder of surprise ran through her body and she tried to suppress it and ignore the incident. But his fingers hadn't touched her neck by accident. She felt their caress, they stroked her neck and slid down to her shoulder and back up again. She went on rolling up the sleeve and felt his eyes fixed on her, examining her reaction. But she didn't know how to react. She wondered if it really gave her pleasure. She had never been attracted to Pesach, she had never dreamed of anyone but the one and only, the unattainable. But nevertheless she wanted to postpone for as long as possible the moment when she would finish rolling up the sleeve and he would be obliged to take his fingers off her neck. The touch of the strange fingers which at the first moment had sent a shiver of surprise through her and given her gooseflesh, began to melt something inside her which had been frozen for a long time. As in a dream she sensed the warmth of the fingers and the softness of their touch and the sound of his warm breath brushing past her and the gleam of his eyes looking straight into her eyes and she knew that she was ready to give her life for these moments. She went on slowly rolling up the sleeve, straightening out every wrinkle in the roll of cloth, and when she passed his elbow she felt the swelling curve of his muscle filling the hollow of the sleeve. She had to make an effort to turn the roll over again, the cloth was so tight against the muscle. His fingers rose from her neck to stroke her cheek. A kind of tenderness welled up in her, a new and unfamiliar tenderness which she had not imagined existed in her and a feeling of gratitude toward this strange boy whom she had never loved and the touch of whose fingers on her neck restored to her as if by magic her lost warmth and the will to live. Suddenly he was very dear to her and she didn't know if there was any way in the world to repay him for this blessing.

She finished rolling up the sleeve, plucked up her courage and looked him in the eye. He took his hand off her shoulder and smiled at her. His wet hair changed his appearance. Instead of the mop of curls falling over his forehead his hair was combed smooth and flat against his head. This hairstyle and his white shirt made him look like a little boy. His green eyes smiled at her with feeling and warmth in an expression she had never seen there before. He placed his second hand on her shoulder, but before she began rolling up the sleeve, she heard him say:

"Naomi, you're the best of them all. You I really love."

Tears immediately welled into her eyes and she couldn't hold them back. She was ashamed of her tears and turned her face aside. He removed his hand from her shoulder, took her chin in his hand and turned her face toward his.

"Why are you crying? I told you I loved you, because you're so good."

"I know," said Naomi and her voice trembled, "It moves me very much."

He embraced her with both arms. She felt his cheek pressed warmly against hers. Her eyes were closed and it seemed to her that she was moving far away from the place where she was standing, far, far away from all the familiar places in each of which she had left something of her disgrace and the torments of her sickness. But suddenly a tremor from outside ran through her. She opened her eyes, saw the lights of the hut and knew that they might be seen. Gently she pushed his face away from hers and took hold of the hand whose sleeve was still unrolled.

"They can see us," said Naomi, "someone might come this way."

"So what?" asked Pesach. He let her roll up his other sleeve.

"You know," he said, "I'm not coming back to the high school any more. I'm quitting school."

It was to be expected. He had failed in the end-of-term examinations in spite of all the efforts to help him. But his announcement now sounded to her new and surprising, very painful.

"You won't see me any more," continued Pesach, "I'm going to work in construction until I'm drafted in a few months' time."

"So the party tonight is also your farewell party," said Naomi. He laughed softly.

She still didn't want to part from him. "This past year was a good one though, wasn't it?" she said. "At least you'll have good memories from this year."

"No," said Pesach. "Not at all."

"Don't you feel happy together with everyone?"

"No," said Pesach. "I'm not together with everyone. I just pretend to be. I'm always seperate. Once I liked being alone, but now I can't any more. Once I didn't care what people said about me and now I hear them talking all the time and I don't know if it's good for me or not. But I know that it's just a game. Everyone plays it and I play it too. And just like it started one day for nothing, it'll end suddenly for nothing too. I don't believe anyone. They're not my friends. I only believe you because you're really good and maybe you really like me. I can feel it. That's why I love you. I didn't want to play the reed at the party, why should I make a fool of myself, but you were so keen for me to bring it and I saw that you were so set on it, so I'm doing it for you."

"In a minute I'll begin to cry again," said Naomi, and she smiled at him and examined his face as she had never dared to do until this minute, as if she wanted to engrave his features in her memory, as if she woud never see them again. "You know, nobody's ever said anything like that to me before, nobody's ever treated me so beautifully and so tenderly. I'm alone too, terribly alone, and I'm not happy. I've never told this to anybody, but I want you to know it. Because after next week we won't see you at school anymore and who knows if we'll ever meet again. Maybe after a long time we'll pass each other in the street like two strangers and hardly say hello. Maybe we'll even be ashamed of this memory. But I'd like, I'd like so very much for you to remember me and to remember this moment when we stood here behind the hut. Because I'll never forget it, never!"

She held his hand tightly and put her other hand on his cheek, to soak up its warmth and to keep the feeling of a contact she had never known before on her hand.

"If you like we can go on meeting after I quit school too," said Pesach.

But Naomi no longer heard what he was saying to her, she looked apprehensively at the lighted hut:

"We have to go back to the hut, soon they'll come to look for me. You go in first and I'll come later. I have to get ready to read the poem," she pointed at the book lying at her feet. He bent down, picked up the book, looked at it for a minute and gave it to her. Then he smiled at her again, walked slowly to the hut and disappeared into the door.

Naomi entered a few minutes later and everyone was dressed and ready for the party. We were still waiting for Yigal and his guests to appear. There were a few minutes to go before the time set for the party to begin and Yigal was a stickler for punctuality, as military discipline, according to him, demanded. And indeed at exactly seven o'clock he entered the hut with the two girl soldiers. They sat on the bed in the center of the semicircle and Eli played *"How good and how pleasant it is for brothers to be together"* on his accordion. We all joined in the singing. After a few more songs Yigal stood up and asked permission to say a few words. He extolled the military importance of the work we had done and its contribution to the security of the state, dwelt on the pleasure it had given him to instruct us and his sorrow at the fact that we were already leaving in the morning. And so that we would all remember these glorious days and take pride in them, each of us would be given a planter's badge to wear on his collar. He took the badges out of a box and called us up one by one to receive them. He pinned the badges on our collars and shook hands with us solemnly. It seemed to me that Pesach looked a little glum. I wouldn't have thought that winning the badge had meant so much to him. When the pinning on of the badges was over, we resumed our singing until Naomi considered the atmosphere had warmed up sufficiently to begin the artistic program. She stood up in her corner (she always sat in the corner at the parties she organized), signaled to Eli to stop playing, and when everybody was quiet she announced:

"Pesach will now play 'Debka Rafiah' for us on the Arab shepherd's reed."

The surprise was effective. Silence fell, interrupted by a bit of clapping and whispers of disbelief. Pesach jumped off the bed, went over to the luggage piled in the corner, opened his bag and took out the instrument. It was a piece of reed as thick as a hosepipe with holes all the way down it. Pesach bounded back to his place, sat down, raised the reed sideways to his mouth, pursed his lips and blew. No sound emerged. He licked his lips with his tongue, pursed them and reapplied them to the hole, set the reed at the required angle and blew again. This time a few weak sounds emerged and after them the air was suddenly split by a loud whistle, crude, shrill and discordant—and that was it. He held the reed in both hands, examined it as if wondering what could have gone wrong, and suddenly his fingers clenched as if to break it, he looked in front of him as if trying to make up his mind whether to break it or not, and a spasm passed through his body as he heard the laughter. A few people burst out laughing, their laughter infected others, and in an instant the whole hut was convulsed by gales of laughter growing louder all the time. Pesach's face reddened. He tried to laugh with us as if he shared the joke, but the fit of laughter shaking the walls of the hut rejected his participation. Pesach's face fell and through the tears of laughter I saw him sitting stunned, dismayed, falling apart bit by bit.

Naomi stood up and tried to silence us. "It's a very difficult instrument to play," she cried as loudly as she could to overcome the noise, "sometimes the notes don't come out quite right at first." As usual in such cases her words only increased the merriment and the laughter grew deafening, rolling and crashing like an avalanche. "Eli!" she cried in despair, "Eli, do something!" Eli who had taken up his position to accompany Pesach's playing, had buried his head in the accordion on his knees and his shoulders shook with laughter. He raised his head and tried to force a serious expression onto his face: "Stop it people," he said, "have a heart. . . ." but his voice broke and bellowed with laughter and his hands shook so much the accordion was in danger of slipping off his knees and crashing to the floor. Naomi sat down in her corner and buried her face in her hands. Yigal and the two soldier girls almost fell off the bed they were sitting on, they were so convulsed with laughter. The laughter went on for a long time, renewing itself whenever it seemed about to die down, until our strength gave out and we ran out of breath. The deep blush which had covered Pesach's face at first disappeared and his face grew pale and stiff. His green cat's eyes gazed strangely and blankly as if they didn't see us, as if he were sitting in another space, remote and undefined. And through the ruins falling wall after wall, fence after fence, under the pressure of that inner force which I believed had worked within him and dictated his external transformation, was exposed the nucleus of that beauty which had revealed itself to us during the past year, in various guises and different degrees. In the final revelation now taking place before my eyes it seemed to me to transcend shape and form, like those things that exist only for the fraction of a second, in a flash of thought; it was a beauty stripped of all form, empty of all expression, denuded of all sensuality, innocent of all external reference, free of all dependence. The pallor of the face and the cold fire smoldering in the green eyes, wider open than usual, the thick lips, slightly apart as if struck dumb forever, emphasized the frozen purity of this beauty, after which only death was possible. And I who had always loved the beauty of the defeated could not take my eyes off Pesach; I had never before seen a beauty comparable to his beauty at those moments.

It took a long time for the moans and gasps, the writhings and twitchings to stop. Gradually the sounds died down. We sat there breathing heavily, too exhausted even to talk. Naomi waited until everyone had calmed down, took her hands off her eyes, stood up and looked at us without speaking, sadly and reproachfully. She asked Pesach: "Do you want to try again?" Again the laughter broke out here and there, inciting us to begin all over again, but this time it did not spread, we had already had enough. Pesach did not reply, he didn't see us, he didn't even turn his head in Naomi's direction. As if hypnotized he went on staring at the same mysterious point with a frozen face. He was not with us.

Naomi reflected for a moment as if trying to make up her mind, her hands trembling as she held the book, but an expression of resolution immediately appeared on her face: the party had to go on as planned. She opened the book of poems, cleared her throat with a slight cough and closed her eyes in concentration. She opened her eyes, looked straight into our eyes and spoke the poem:

Today my eyes in a double suddenness
have opened toward You.
I am innocent, Lord.
When the sun grazes on the water,
I remember
I was born in your presence twins.

In the first verse her agitation still interfered with her concentration and her reading lacked the confidence and feeling we had come to expect from her. She paused, glanced at the book, raised her eyes to us again and declaimed:

It is evening now. You have clouded the windows.
You have put out the light,
darkened the landscape.
For the son You love, Your only one,
dies in me—he whom my hand smote
in the meadows.

I am innocent, Lord.
Striking him slowly, slowly,
I dragged him from mother and home
to put him up for sale.
I took off his shirt.
I waited for his tears.
And as I bound his arms,
he smiled dumbly.

I always knew in my heart
he was dearer to You than I.
He, only he, was favored in Your eyes.
I leaned over him like a nursemaid
as he lay in his cradle of pain,
and my harmonica eased him with my tunes.

Her voice suddenly choked and her fists clenched round the two halves of the open book. I saw her short fingers whiten as they tightened on the covers, she coughed, as if to clear her throat again, and went on reciting.

> *When Your strange night opened to call me,*
> *I escaped toward it,*
> *cloaked by its song.*
> *My struggling brother,*
> *my brother who was going to die,*
> *was left unconfessed, without water.*
>
> *Today my soul desires*
> *to dwell in You, forgotten.*
> *You are a dense forest to me,*
> *oppressive and sad.*
> *If only You could see*
> *how between night and dawn,*
> *my hands plead at Your door—*
> *to let me return.*

Her voice broke and tears flooded her eyes. She couldn't go on reading. For a moment she stood before us weeping and looking at us, perhaps accusing, perhaps begging us to save her, and then she closed the book and returned to her place in the corner.

Arik went up to her. He tried to comfort her but she couldn't stop sobbing, or pronounce the words she was trying to say: It's all my fault. Rachel sat down next to her and put her arms around her and Naomi wept inconsolably in her embrace. Yigal looked worried and the two soldier girls, like experienced older sisters, went up to offer advice and assistance. When she recovered Naomi asked Arik to read his skits and go on running the party in her place.

Arik stood before us at a loss. The transition from the hilarious, liberating laughter after Pesach's performance to Naomi's weeping was so sharp that it had plunged us all into a tense uneasiness. Arik didn't have the heart to read his skits. He looked at Eli and asked him to strike up for another round of community singing, hoping that this would restore our spirits. At first the singing was weak and hesitant but gradually it grew louder and more lively. As we sang we saw Pesach get up, walk to the door, and go outside. Naomi started up in alarm and made as if to follow him, perhaps to persuade him to return, to try to patch things up, but Arik who was sitting next to her quickly seized her hand and pulled her down again. Then he whispered something in her ear and she was persuaded to remain where she was.

By the time Arik stood up to read his skits the tension had relaxed and we were ready to laugh again. He read "The Anthem of the Little Polish Refugees" which he had put to the music of a well-known song, and afterward we sang the refrain with him. He read an amusing description of a day of planting, adding clever imitations of a number of characters in our group, and not sparing Yigal the instructor and his stories about the Pardes Hanna Agricultural School either. Yigal responded with laughter and the good humor appropriate to such occasions. After Arik concluded his skits and imitations happiness returned to our hearts and we began to feel hungry. The word was given and we all rushed to the buffet.

When we had satisfied our hunger Eli played the "hora" and we made a circle and danced round him enthusiasically. And once more there rose around me the smell of sweat and dust which always accompanied our dancing and which has remained in my memory to this day as the smell of my youth. Yigal and the two soldier girls joined the circle too and shouted rhythmically with us: "*The haystacks of Mizra are burning!*" From the circle I saw Arik sitting with Naomi on one of the beds, loyal to the old comradeship between them. The expression on his face was sadder, more serious and mature than any I had ever seen there before. A great affection for Arik welled up in me and banished the jollity of the dance from my heart. I left the circle, stood to one side and looked at him, examining his face which was quiet, intelligent and very thoughtful. What was it about this face which so astonished me? It was no longer the same Arik I had known for so many years. As if in those moments a mask had been torn off him, and the new face radiated a powerful, reserved kind of inner serenity, and a pure and very beautiful loneliness. Was he aware of the change which had suddenly taken place in him? I wanted to go up to him, to sit beside him, to be close to him, to share his thoughts, to share in the loyal comradeship between him and Naomi, in the transformation which had taken place in him, to be given a place in his world, which I was afraid had been closed to me with the changing of his face. Was Arik's friendship lost to me? His friendship had never been so precious to me as in these moments, when he was revealed to me as a new person who had travelled a long road and reached his destination, far beyond my horizons. I drew closer to them and they stopped talking. Naomi gave me her sad, apologetic, defeated smile. I sat down beside them and all three of us were silent. The sounds of the singing and stamping feet of the dancers sounded to me now, sitting outside the circle, like the beat of a different tune, unfamiliar but stubborn and sweeping, which was well expressed by Naomi's smile. We've all been defeated, I said to myself, vanquished in a war whose outcome was determined in advance. I looked at my friends dancing in a circle and from their noisy merriment and their flushed, sweating faces a cry rose in my ears: To go home, back to memory. When I looked at Arik it seemed to me that he had gone further than anyone else: he looked to me like someone who had thrown in the sponge, surrendered, renounced everything. Was this the meaning of the transformation that had taken place in him and given his face the expression of purity and power which so attracted me and so frightened me? I wanted to say something to him but I didn't know the words which would bring the old Arik back to the new face. Naomi said: "Won't you go to him now?" And Arik replied: "It's not necessary, it won't do any good." I knew they were talking about Pesach. I remembered what Arik had once said about Pesach and the taming of a wild animal, when he had predicted one of three possibilities. Had he been right this time too? I wanted to remind him of it. I looked at him and saw that his face was unresponsive. He wasn't interested in talking to me. I wondered where Pesach was and what he was doing. Only Arik knew that he was sitting by himself in the sapling shed, in the grip of forces beyond human control.

Yigal and the girl soldiers took their leave of us. It was late and the party was over. We opened the windows to air the hut and began getting ready to go to bed. The girls cleared away the remains of the refreshments, the trestle tables were dismantled and the beds returned to their places. After a while the blankets were hung on the rope partitioning the hut in two, but in spite of the weariness of our bodies our spirits were still agitated and nobody wanted to sleep. We lay in bed and talked until complaints rose from the girls' quarters that we were stopping them from falling asleep. Eli got up and switched off the light. Before he could cover himself with his blankets again the door of the hut opened. Pesach entered, paused for a moment on the threshold, went up to the switch and put on the light.

He looked pale and rigid as a sleepwalker. Slowly he walked to his bed and stood next to it to get undressed. He took off his white shirt and his undershirt and his shoes and his trousers and his underpants and stood there quite naked. Then he walked slowly to the partition and pulled down the blankets, went up to the light switch of the girls' quarters and put the light on there too. One of the girls cried out in alarm. All of them lay awake in their beds without moving, their eyes wide open. He heard nothing and saw no one. His eyes were cold and cruel. Slowly he walked naked up and down the hut, from end to end, like a caged wild animal, back and forth in a circle, faster and faster until his pacing turned to running, to a panic-stricken gallop. There was silence in the hut, all we could hear was the thudding of his bare feet on the floor and the grunting of his rhythmic pants. He stopped suddenly and looked at his groin. We saw the big erection sticking out of the bush of red hair. He cupped his hands around his mouth and uttered the hyena's scream of laughter, and he began to run again, and the screaming didn't stop, the long, high-pitched, terrible howl of laughter spun around us and rolled from end to end of the hut, as if it wasn't coming out of his throat but reaching us from some place far away, a place which we would never know. Gradually his figure grew blurred until only the red patch was visible, like a flame circling swiftly round us, threatening to flare up and spread and light a conflagration that would consume everything in its blaze.

A NOTE ON THE AUTHOR

Yehoshua Kenaz was born in 1937 and lives in Tel Aviv,
where he writes in Hebrew and works on the editorial staff
of the daily newspaper *Ha'aretz*. He is also a film and the-
ater critic, and a translator from the French. He has won
several awards for literature, including the Bialik Prize, the
Prime Minister Eshkol Prize, Histadrut's Alterman Prize,
the Agnon Prize, and the Bar Ilam University Newman
Prize. Two of his previous books have been published in
English: *After the Holidays,* in 1982, and *The Way To the
Cats,* in 1994.

❀

A NOTE ON THE BOOK

The text for this book was composed by Steerforth Press
using a digital version of Sabon, a typeface designed by Jan
Tschichold and first cut and cast at the Stempel Foundry in
1964. The book was printed on acid free papers and bound
by Princeton Academic Press of Lawrenceville, New Jersey.